CW00571408

Happy Lies the Heart

By

Emma Carney

Emma Carney (signature)

The copyright of this book is the sole property of www.michaelparker books.com. No part of this book can be reproduced or copied without the express permission the publisher.

Dedicated to the memory of Patricia Anne Parker

14/01/1942 – 18/08/2020

Book jacket by:thebooktypesetters.com

Chapter 1

Jenny drove the last spike into the ground, straightened up and rubbed her hands together with a smile of satisfaction. The Gazebo was finally up and anchored securely. She dropped the hammer into a tool bag and went back to her car thankful the organisers had allowed the stall holders to park close enough to offload their merchandise. The sun hadn't quite lifted its head, but there was a promise of good weather, which made the prospect of spending most of the day behind a stall more encouraging; something that encouraged Jenny enormously.

Now that she had erected the Gazebo, the Wendy House as she preferred to call it, she was able to set up her table, pile the books and treats on, and set about making it as attractive and presentable as possible. It wasn't something Jenny was used to doing, but her friend, Sue, who she had known since nursery school (was it that long ago?), had been persuaded by Jenny to push the boat out and pay for a pitch, as exorbitant a price as it was.

Jenny was at the Chichester Revival Festival. It was six o'clock in the morning and all stallholders had been warned to have their vehicles moved to the designated car park before seven o'clock. The area for the small, niche businesses had been set aside from the main show area of the festival, where large marquises, jazz bands, restaurants and all manner of shops were lined up ready for the weekend.

It wasn't Jenny's first time at the festival; she'd been before, but she was looking forward to having a spell wandering round the exhibits and side shows while Sue looked after the stall. Soon there would be all kinds of people there, many dressed in the style of the roaring twenties and some in uniforms from both wars. There would be people dressed in the style popular among the afficionados of Jazz and Swing, strutting their stuff to the swing bands that always attracted both dancers and spectators. Old styles, new styles — it was all promising to be a great Revival weekend.

Jenny walked away from the stall into the area through which all the foot traffic would be passing and stood there to admire her handiwork. The stall looked cheerful and colourful, loaded with pretty bunting, small bowls of coloured sweets, trinkets for the children because, after all, it was all about children's books — something Sue had been doing since she was quite young. Her dream was to become a traditionally published, bestselling author.

After admiring her handiwork for a few minutes, Jenny looked to the left at the double size Gazebo, literally dwarfing her three metre tent, and slowly filling up with what looked like spare motor parts. There were two men putting this all together, their language was a bit choice, but Jenny wondered what else she could expect — men would be men. It was as though they were unaware she was standing just a few yards away. Either that or they didn't care.

On the other side of her stall was another six metre monster which, together with her neighbour seemed to squash her lovely, lively creation into little more than a pretty box.

She frowned, shaking her head a little and walked back to towards her car, ready to move it back to the reserved parking area. She had to walk past the large gazebo. She glanced at the two men as one of them called to her. They looked like brothers because of their striking resemblance to each other. Handsome too.

"Morning, darling. Lovely day."

Jenny glared at him. "I'm not your darling."

He made a mocking bow. "Sorry love."

"And I'm not your love either."

He turned to his friend and muttered something uncomplimentary, but loud enough for Jenny to hear. They both laughed.

Jenny ignored the barb and climbed into her car. She wished Sue was with her, but her friend had suffered a minor injury at work and needed her dressing changed that morning. Jenny had bravely stepped in to save Sue's big day.

Jenny parked her car and walked over to one of the early stalls that were selling hot drinks and snacks. She picked up a coffee to go and walked back to her stall. She sat down in a comfortable director's chair, picked up one of the children's books and began flicking through the pages.

"Good morning."

She looked up. It was one of the men who had spoken to her earlier and been rebuffed. She banged her eyes and looked down at the book.

"No good morning back, then?" he asked.

Jenny put the book down and looked up at him again.

"Good morning."

"That's better. My name's Simon. I won't eat you; I promise."

Jenny was immediately taken by the man's good looks and his beautiful blue eyes. She felt a change in her heart's rhythm, and it unsettled her. She cleared her throat and coughed softly.

"Pleased to meet you," she said, and picked up her coffee. "I suppose we're going to be neighbours all day." She said it with enough tired enthusiasm to make it clear to him that she wasn't interested in striking up a conversation.

"I'm sorry about my brother this morning: he's like that. Gets on with everybody."

"Oh, I thought it was you."

Simon smiled. It was a lovely smile and another disarming moment for Jenny. "He's my twin. We might look alike but we don't behave the same."

Jenny put her head down again. "Thank goodness for that," she said softly. "I'm not sure I could handle the attention."

"So, what are you selling?"

She couldn't stop the sound of amazement that came out when she answered. "Isn't that obvious?" she said bluntly, lifting the book up. "Children's books."

"Oh." He picked up one of the books. "You write these yourself? He looked at the name on the front cover. "Sue?"

"My name's not Sue; it's Jenny."

He put the book down, making sure it was neatly aligned with the others in the pile. "Well hello, Jenny. It's a pen name then." He arched his eyebrows in a gesture that said he'd worked out her little secret.

He was becoming a nuisance and Jenny wanted him to go back to his stall and leave her alone. As much as she liked looking at him, she didn't like his persistence. She imagined he would be pestering her all day long because she was sure as hell he wouldn't be selling too many car parts or whatever they were.

"Look," she said wearily. "I am doing my friend a big favour. She had an accident at work and needs to be at the clinic this morning to have her dressing changed. This stall was to be her big day, and she paid a lot of money for the pitch. She's the writer and was really looking forward to being here. So I'm doing it for her. As a big favour," she added.

"That's nice of you. Is she okay?"

Jenny eyes hooded over. "Yes, she's fine. Thank you."

"Have you done this before? Selling books, I mean."

Jenny shook her head. "Not on my own," she told him, still reluctant to get into a conversation. "I've helped Sue on occasions. Nothing too grand though."

"Will she be coming today?"

"I hope so."

He leaned forward, both hands on the edge of the table.

Jenny noticed they were big hands. Strong looking. She imagined them on her arms… She stopped her mind from dwelling on what it would be like.

"Let me say this then," he said. "If you want to go off for a coffee or spend a penny and your friend isn't here, I'll mind the stall for you." He straightened and opened his palms. Jenny's pulse lifted a notch.

"Thank you," she said. "That's good of you. I hope that won't be necessary."

He smiled and winked at her. "Any time," he said in such a way that suggested he wasn't talking about minding the stall, and walked away leaving Jenny with a rueful smile dancing on her lips; one that she was doing hard to suppress.

She tried to get absorbed into the book she was reading

7

but couldn't help an occasional glance over at the two men. She noticed the sweatshirts they were wearing had a fancy engineering logo beneath the words 'Trojan Racing'.

She went back to the book, but try as she might, she couldn't stop lifting her head and sneaking another look. Eventually she put the book down and pulled her phone out from her handbag, She searched for Trojan Racing and came up with a surprisingly full web Page. Trojan Racing was a subsidiary of Trojan Design Concepts, Trojan Satellite Systems and Trojan Aviation.

She turned her phone off and frowned: what was a massive organisation like Trojan doing with a pop-up stall at the festival? And what were those two jokers doing working for a conglomerate like that, she wondered. She decided they must be salesmen or something. No way would any executives been seen dead on what amounted to little more than a glorious car-boot stall.

Then she realised that was exactly what she was doing, and immediately felt sorry for Sue, inferring her children's books were only fit for a car-boot.

Suddenly a shadow fell across her book. She looked up and saw Simon standing there.

"Sorry to bother you, but would you keep an eye on our stall while we go for pi…" He dropped his head. "Sorry, it nearly slipped out. While we go to the toilet. Please?"

Jenny could hardly refuse as she was going nowhere; all she had to do was stay put and read her book.

"Yes, of course. I won't be able to sell anything for you though."

He screwed his nose up. "Don't worry; there aren't enough people here yet, and no-one will buy anything anyway." And with that he turned and called over to his

8

brother.

"We're okay," he shouted. "All friends now."

Jenny opened her mouth to say something but decided to let it drop. There was no point in getting annoyed. Eventually the day would begin, Sue would be here and she could look forward to the kind of humour and company she could enjoy rather than that which those two apes engaged in.

Chapter 2

It was mid-morning before Sue arrived. She was breathless from hurrying and apologised for not being there to help Jenny set up.

"I'm so sorry you had to do this for me, Jenny. I was really looking forward to the two of us putting all this together." She looked over the stall, casting an experienced eye on the way Jenny had set it all up. "You did wonderfully: it's fabulous."

"Not bad for a beginner, eh?"

"Did it all on your own? Didn't need any help from those two gorgeous hunks over there?"

Jenny puffed her cheeks out. "Positive bores, the pair of them. I think they're more interested in chatting me up that doing any work."

"You've spoken to them then?"

Jenny snorted. "Hardly a conversation," she said. She pointed to Simon. "That one is Simon, the other is his brother, Harry — twin brother so he tells me. They work for Trojan something or other. Couple of salesmen I think. And typical salesman judging by their manners and behaviour. Like a couple of schoolboys, the pair of them."

"Trojan Engineering?"

Jenny nodded. "Yes, I think that's what they said. It's on their banner, so it must be right. Why?"

"Big firm, that. Global I think."

Jenny snorted. "Well, they need to retrain their salesmen — teach them some manners."

Sue laughed. "My, my, Jenny Paige, you do have a grump against them." She looked over at the two brothers who were chatting away happily to a couple of punters

10

who had turned up at their stall. "They look like fun from where I'm standing," she said with a glint in her eye.

Jenny punched her gently on the arm. "Any more of that and you'll need another dressing change."

Sue laughed and pulled a bottle from her large shopping bag. "I bought a sweetener," she said as she held a bottle of wine up. "Might cheer you up. Shall I pour?"

"Not too much; we must remember we're driving home tonight."

Sue smiled as she poured the wine into a couple of glasses. "Unless we need to ask someone nearby for a lift."

Jenny took her drink and sipped it. "You're incorrigible," she said.

"Morning, girls!"

Jenny put her hand on her forehead and moaned out loud. Sue turned and looked over as Simon walked over to them.

"Early morning prandials?" he asked. "Are we sharing?"

"We?" Jenny said stuffily. "Who's we?"

Sue waved her away with a flutter of her hand. "I can't possibly give a stranger a drink, can I?" she said with a coy look on her face.

"I'm Simon," he said to Sue. "And that's my brother, Harry." He pointed over to Harry who touched his forehead and bowed graciously, grinning like a Cheshire cat."

"Now we are properly introduced —" He stopped abruptly. "Of course, oh I'm sorry; Jenny hasn't introduced us yet."

Sue flashed a knowing glance at Jenny. "I'm Sue, Jenny's lifelong friend."

"Pleased to meet you, Jenny's lifelong friend. I understand you are a children's author."

Sue demurred. Jenny didn't think it suited her, but she was obviously falling under the spell of Simon's disarming nature, lovely hands, and beautiful blue eyes. She cursed herself for going through a short inventory of the man's undisputable good points.

"Thank you," Sue answered. "Not world class though."

He looked at her steadily. "I bet you are to someone." His expression changed and softened a little. "At home?"

Jenny stood up suddenly. "Oh my goodness," she said. "I'm off to the toilet. Hope you sell some books while I'm gone."

Simon looked on staggered as Jenny extracted herself from behind the stall.

"Don't be long," he called after her. Then he turned to Sue. "She got the hump or something?"

Sue laughed. "That's my Jenny. I know what's wrong, but I can't share it with you. She'd kill me."

"God forbid." He moved closer. "So what about that drink? And is there anyone at home?"

"It's too early for a drink. And yes, there is someone at home."

"If it's too early, why are you drinking?"

Sue looked at her glass. It was empty. "Closing time," she said. "Might open up later."

His eyes widened and a smile gathered at the corner of his mouth. "I'll look forward to that," he said softly and leaned closer.

"Simon!"

He turned round and glanced quickly over his shoulder at his brother. "Just when it was getting interesting," he said, and straightened up. "Looks like I have something else to engage me." He put his finger tip to his lips and touched Sue on hers. "Keep that for later."

Sue watched him as he walked the short distance to his stall. His brother gave him a knowing look. Sue grinned and turned away, back to her books and her mind in something of a whirl.

It was several minutes before Jenny returned. "Well?" she muttered as she slid behind the stall and flopped down into the director's chair. "Hooked up with lover boy yet?"

"What would you care?"

"I care about you, Sue. Men like that have no scruples and only one thing on their mind."

"Who says it's only the men?"

Jenny's mouth opened wide. "Sue Knight! I can't believe you said that."

Sue laughed. "We're not getting any younger," she trilled.

"That's a cliché, you know it is. Besides, neither of us has reached thirty yet; too busy making a career for ourselves."

Sue sat down in the other Director's chair. "Well, my career isn't exactly a shooting firework of success. Hairdressing is my job; writing is my career. Well, I'd like to think it was," she added.

Jenny pinched her lips together and nodded her agreement. "And the career isn't going too well, is it?"

"That's what I said. I'm a bottom feeder," she told her, and Jenny burst out laughing.

"Oh, sorry, I couldn't help it. Just don't tell glamour boy over there you're a bottom feeder." She stifled her laughter and apologised again.

"What about you, Jen?" Sue asked. "Where's your advertising career going?"

Jenny worked for an advertising and marketing company. She'd been there since finishing University and had hoped for significant movement through the ranks as time progressed, but the stumbling block for Jenny was her boss, Kathleen Johnson — KJ as she liked to be called: it sounded strong, important, and just a little out of reach to mere mortals. They didn't get on; it was as simple as that.

Jenny drew in a deep breath before answering Sue's question. "I'm on notice, I think. One more chance or I'm out. At least, that's what it feels like."

Sue looked concerned. "Really? You never told me."

Jenny shrugged. "You always believed in me, Sue. Always held me up like a beacon of success to your friends. But the truth is, I'm swimming in a pool of sharks. Sometimes I wish I was a bottom feeder too, then maybe the sharks would take no notice of me."

"Which means you would never get on. All the time you want to stay low means you have nothing to aim for. And if that's the case, you'll hit the target every time."

Jenny's eyes opened wide. "Wow, that's some philosophy coming from you. Where did you get that one from?"

"I'm not all perms, rinses and blow dries you know," she said a little haughtily.

"Blow jobs maybe," Jenny chuckled. She touched Sue on the knee. "Sorry love, that was a bit coarse."

Sue ignored the jibe, but it did trigger some pleasant images with Simon. She put on an affected sigh. "If only," she murmured.

They were both laughing when someone came up to the

14

stall and began looking at the books. Jenny let Sue take the lead because, after all, she was the author. She stood up with Sue, hands behind her back and fingers tightly crossed. It took ten minutes of talk, admiration of the books, a short summary of her writing and how many books had she published before the woman said she would be back once she'd made a tour of the other stalls. That meant she wouldn't be returning.

Sue dropped into her chair with a bump. "So, now we've seen how my career is taking off, what about you, Jenny? Any movement, or are you really on notice?"

Jenny was really disappointed having witnessed Sue's brave attempts to squeeze a few bob out of a punter. She wondered how she would fare herself when it came to selling the potentially huge contract that was in the pipeline. She decided to tell Sue about it, make it seem as though the challenge would be similar to selling a book. It was a product after all.

"My boss has the chance of a significant contract lined up with a major company. The department's been working on it for some time. Trouble is that the guy who was tasked to sell the contract was knocked off his bloody electric scooter and ended up in hospital."

Sue started giggling.

"Stop it!"

Sue apologised and stopped giggling. "Executive marketing director gets knocked of his executive scooter. Or was it a 'pool' scooter."

That did it; she collapsed in a fit of laughing and almost fell off the chair. Jenny couldn't help but grin, and then she too started laughing.

Eventually the giggling episode subsided and Jenny was

able to continue.

"The advertising and marketing department is short staffed because of sickness. The pandemic didn't help and we're still having people pull a sickie with long covid." She said it with a slight sneer. "So, it seems that because of my longevity in the job, I have been given the opportunity to make or break the company. Or myself for that matter."

"And do you know who the big company is that you will be dealing with? You know, the one who will treat you like the coming Messiah and fall on their knees that you were chosen to bring this golden opportunity to their doors?"

Jenny stooped and picked up her bag. She flipped it open. "I've got their card here somewhere. Plus a whole shed load of information at home." She rummaged through the bag until she pulled out a card with a soft shout of acclamation and held it up.

Suddenly her arm dropped on to her lap and she looked up at Sue with a dour expression clouding her face.

"Oh my god," she said. "It's only fucking Trojan Engineering."

Chapter 3

Jenny closed the door of her flat and started jogging towards East Street where she planned to turn and run along the inner ring road which would bring her round to the lovely Priory Park. From there she would head towards the precincts before turning back to her flat in The Hornet. She had Kendrick Lamar singing 'Doves in the Wind' on Bluetooth earpieces and hoped that, and the jogging, would expel the memory of her encounter with the 'motor mouths' as she called them, and the awful fact that she had forgotten the name of the Trojan Engineering Company when asked by Sue at the Chichester Revival.

What bothered Jenny was that she had managed to forget the name of the company despite the fact she had been working alongside the poor man who had been knocked off his electric scooter. Although no more than a peripheral figure, it wouldn't have done for her boss to learn that Jenny didn't really have her eye on the ball.

She thought back to that moment as she jogged through the sparsely filled streets, breathing in the fresh, slightly cold September air, and could see Sue falling about laughing over Scooter man's demise. It brought a smile to her face.

She got back to her flat, had a warm-down in the kitchen, made an espresso and dived thankfully into the shower. Breakfast was a probiotic drink and a nutbar. Jenny was nothing if not fit and healthy. She may not have had the brains or advertising skills of Scooter man, but she was all the advertising department had, although she doubted very much that the firm depended on her as much as she depended on them.

After her breakfast, Jenny brushed her teeth and dressed, deciding to wear a pink, two piece blazer office suit with wide leg pants. She matched up her imitation, brown Armani handbag with colour coordinated, high heeled shoes. She checked herself over in the mirror and was felt she was ready, and looking confident enough, to deal with her boss.

As Jenny walked to her office in North Street, she thought again about the events at the Revival and Sue's meagre sales at the book stall. Sue took it all in her stride though. She would say it's all about making a connection and getting your name out there. But the facts were, she didn't sell enough to cover her expenses.

As for the apes who seemed more interested in chatting her and Sue up than behaving properly; they were beyond a joke. Although she admitted grudgingly to herself that the one who called himself Simon was rather good looking. In another time and space continuum, she would like to have tested the water with that one. Sue on the other hand looked ready to fall into bed with him. She affected a shudder at the idea of being that easy.

Then she recalled some of her more spectacular failures at lovemaking, particularly when some young teenage boy was fumbling with her bra straps and making her laugh. Or some more knowledgeable, careful young men who knew how to pick their way through the minefield that was adolescent courting. She'd banged a few in her time, but none of them ever really clicked. She was pushing thirty as well. It wouldn't be too long before she was heading into the old maid category.

The double front, iron doors to the building in which the marketing company was situated, had been locked back in the open position. There was a desk just inside the front entrance where a security guard was stationed. He was in uniform. Sometimes the guard was a woman. Their task was to point visitors in the right direction and generally answer questions for the benefit of those office dwellers who didn't know the answers. A boring job, Jenny thought each time she passed through those open doors.

Jenny acknowledged the incumbent with a nod as she walked by. She never knew their names, which was something the security people took notice of and marked it down mentally should any of those type need anything at any time. Life could be made difficult for those who thought they were of a higher station in life.

She took the lift up to the third floor and walked briskly into the company offices, went straight to coffee machine, and bought an espresso.

"In here when you've opened your desk please Jenny!"

Her boss always referred to her staff starting work as 'opening their desks'. Jenny glance over as Kathleen Johnson disappeared into her glass atrium. It could be a scary place at times, scarier than the conference room, particularly when her boss was on a crusade.

Jenny went to her desk, booted up her computer, entered her password and pulled up the web Page for Trojan Engineering Proposals. She scanned the relevant points, finished her coffee, and walked boldly up to the ornate glass door. She pushed it open and checked to make sure her boss was ready for her, which she was of course, and stepped into the room.

And what was to turn out to be the worst time of her life was about to begin.

***

"Sit down, Jenny."

Her boss pointed to the only chair available. It was opposite the desk and far enough away to make anyone sitting there feel disconnected. It was an old trick: a psychology employed by bosses, rulers, dictators (under which category Kathleen Johnson fitted snugly), and any other charlatan who wanted to piss their minions off.

"Are you ready for this?"

Jenny nodded. Her insides were having a tossing competition, but she had to ignore it. She nodded briefly. "I'm fully prepared. I spent the entire weekend going through the figures, the marketing plan, costings, schedules…"

"Yes, yes, I wouldn't have expected anything less." Her boss stabbed the words at her like a machine gun going off. "But are you prepared?" She tapped the side of her head. "Here."

Jenny had lied about the weekend of course. Her and Sue got pissed on Saturday evening once they'd got back from the festival. It seemed like a good idea and took Sue's mind off the fact that she still couldn't give up her day job. Sue couldn't manage the following day and decided not to bother going back to her stall because she felt unwell, and her injury was playing her up, so Jenny did the only thing she could and offered to go back and wrap it all up for her. It meant bumping into motor mouth and his brother again, but what the hell? It was a favour for a friend.

She sat staring at her boss and allowed her mind to morph back to the events of the previous day, shutting out the rat-a-tat narrative about selling and selling big. As her boss slammed her hand down on the desk to make a point, Jenny thought of Simon's hands.

20

***

"Well, you're back. Good morning, Jenny."

Jenny made the effort and returned the greeting but had no wish to add anything..

"Where's Sue?"

"She's not well, so she's staying at home."

"And leaving you to do all the selling?"

Jenny swept her hands over the empty table. "No books. We're done. I'm going to wrap it up."

"Where are the books?"

"In my car. Sue couldn't park in the traders car park because she got here late yesterday, so we put them all in my car last night when we packed up. When I'm cleared away, I'll be taking everything back to Sue's lock-up."

He walked over and came up beside her. As soon as he took a step, Jenny felt her whole body tingle. It was brief, but it she felt it. She could smell his aftershave. It had that macho smell about it: some kind of chemical that animals emit before coupling. She thought it was more to do with animals anyway, but whatever it was, it was a good trick and it worked. She immediately wanted to nuzzle up to him and check the fragrance but sadly she had to give up on that idea.

"Do you want a hand?"

She didn't look at him when she answered. The truth was that she might want to keep looking, and that just wouldn't do.

"No, I'm fine," she said breezily. "I can manage, thank you."

He touched her briefly on the elbow. Her eyes hooded over and she couldn't stop herself taking a short breath.

"Look, I'm not asking you to go to bed with me; I'm

21

just offering to help pack your Gazebo and stuff away." He waited for her to say something, then shrugged and turned away."

"Yes," Jenny said suddenly, realising what a dork she was. "I'm sorry. Yes, that would be nice. Thank you." She waved her hand over the half empty space. "There's just the table and the gazebo really. The cardboard boxes aren't needed. They can go in the bin"

He looked round and called over to his brother who was watching him intently. Simon gave him a finger, making sure Jenny didn't see it. Then he turned round. "Right, let's move the easy stuff out and I'll take the gazebo down for you.

It took less than thirty minutes, and as Jenny closed the boot lid of her car, she suddenly felt disappointed that there was nothing left to do. She turned to face him.

"Well, Simon, thank you again,"

He smiled and shook his head. "Wasn't that painful, was it?"

She grinned sheepishly. "No, and thanks again."

"Before you go," he said. "Can I have your number?"

Jenny couldn't answer straight away. She fumbled mentally, then came up with the wrong answer and tried to hide her awkwardness with a coy smile. "I can't I'm afraid; I already have a boyfriend."

His expression softened. "Ah well. In that case, perhaps a kiss?"

She turned her face towards him. He kissed her gently on the cheek.

"It was nice knowing you, Jenny. Stay safe."

He went back to his brother. Jenny watched him go and then climbed into her car. She started the engine but sat there for a moment trying to compose herself. Then she slammed the wheel with both hands.

"Why did you lie to him you stupid bitch!" she shouted. "Bloody fool."

She looked into the rear view mirror, then turned just in time to see Simon throw his arms around a woman, give her a hug, and kiss her fondly.

Jenny's heart sank and she shook her head slowly from side to side, shoved the gear stick forward and pulled away from what could have been an interesting and exciting future.

Chapter 4

Jenny left her boss's office, the woman's stern words ringing in her ears: words of caution and advice garnered from years of experience as she liked to impress upon her staff. She gathered up her briefcase stuffed with a pile of papers covering every aspect of the marketing plan and walked out of the rear of the building to the waiting taxi.

Jenny had managed to cover some research into Trojan Engineering. The company was based about ten miles from Chichester, situated in a relatively new industrial area that some of the local newspapers had dubbed as West Sussex's own Silicon Valley. There were a number of high tech companies there including Rolls Royce's new technology and logistics centre, and this lent itself to the image created by the media.

The driver dropped Jenny off in front of the impressive, glass fronted entrance to Trojan Design Concepts. She stepped out of the taxi and stood there for a moment as the taxi pulled away, admiring the beauty of the modern architecture. Her mind went back to the motor stall at the festival. She couldn't see the connection, but it was going to be interesting for her to find out. She wondered about the Company name: Trojan Design Concepts. She didn't recall seeing that in any of the online research she'd completed, but there was nothing she could do about that, so she tucked it away to the back of her mind.

She wondered if she would bump into Simon again, but then decided he was probably working inside the factory: a mechanic or something like that. And his brother, Harry, too no doubt. Just thinking about Simon brought her out in goosebumps. She chuckled to herself, took a deep breath, and walked through the opening created by the automatic doors.

Here goes, she thought, and crossed her fingers tightly.

The reception area was sleek, beautiful, and showed class. At the curved reception desk sat a young, lovely looking woman, and beside her an equally attractive man. The young woman looked up as Jenny walked across to the desk.

"Good morning!" She seemed to sing it as she beamed a beautiful smile at Jenny. "How can I help you?"

Jenny had her business card ready. "K.J. Marketing," she said, laying her card on the desk. "I'm Jenny Paige. I have an appointment with Mr. Daines."

The receptionist smiled. "One moment please." She pushed a couple of buttons on her phone base. "Miss Paige for you Mister Daines. You'll come down? Thank you." She looked up and grinned. "Please take a seat. Mister Daines will be down immediately."

Jenny spun slowly on her heel and walked over to the leather chairs positioned around a low table. There were several magazines there. The backdrop to this waiting area was a Trojan logo rolled over what looked like a high speed racing car. Jenny thought of the stall at Chichester. It made her wonder.

A couple of minutes after sitting down, she heard the soft hiss as the lift doors opened and a tall man dressed in a sharply cut business suit stepped into the reception area.

For a brief moment, Jenny didn't recognise him.

"Good morning, Miss Paige. Or should I say, Jenny? How nice to see you again."

It was Simon.

***

Jenny was still in shock when Simon showed her into his luxurious office with a beautiful view over the rolling hills of the South Downs countryside. She'd muttered some indecipherable greeting when he walked up to her and shook her hand. It was all she could do to control herself. She wanted to collapse in hysterics, run a mile, reach up and kiss him, and everything else that came roaring into her mind. But all she could manage was a weak 'Oh, hello Simon, fancy meeting you again.'

He smiled. She thought it looked a bit smug, but what else could it be? He directed her towards the lift and acknowledged the receptionist who seemed to melt the moment he did that. Jenny knew the feeling.

The short ride to the upper floor was done in silence. Jenny could imagine what was going through Simon's mind because she'd been unable to hide her surprise and astonishment. He'd be pumped up with visions of high fiving his brother Harry. *Yeah, man, got her!* She hoped not, but she'd been so abject in failing to hide her feelings, she wondered how on earth she was going to pull off the marketing deal. That's when she realised that her boss should have been there.

She took a couple of slow, silent deep breaths and made every effort to calm her nerves and her wildly beating heart.

"Would you like a cup of coffee, Miss Paige? Or tea? Water?"

"No thanks," she croaked. Then she cleared her throat. "I'm fine."

"Can I call you Jenny?"

She felt herself slump internally and knew she was

going to blow the whole thing. "Well, you managed yesterday, so…" She opened her hands. "Please do."

He leaned back in his chair, brought his hands together and rested them on his lap. "Surprised?"

She nodded. "I certainly didn't expect to…" she paused, looking for the right words.

"Find a stall holder working at a place like this?"

She smiled. "I suppose so. Yes."

"Profiling?"

She frowned. "Profiling? What do you mean?"

He leaned forward. "I'm teasing, Jenny. You see a couple of guys running a stall with motor parts and put them into a box, a compartment. We all do it."

"But motor parts?"

"We have a racing team here. Part experimental, part fun. My brother and I often drive at the Revival. We have a concept car which we find useful for all manner of things."

"You're racing drivers?"

"It's a hobby: nothing too serious."

"But you weren't racing."

He laughed. "We lost the toss. Two of our colleagues drove instead of us. Imagine, you could have met Charlotte and Gabby. That's Gabriela by the way. They would have been working the stall if they'd lost."

"They…" The question drifted away.

He nodded. "Two very clever design engineers who also happen to be useful racing drivers."

Jenny realised the conversation was drifting. She had to remember she was there on business. She could see her boss tapping the side of her head warning her to stay sharp, stay focussed.

"Well," she said, all business like. "It's nice to

27

reminisce, but I'm here on business, so perhaps we should concentrate on that?"

He nodded. "Of course. So, why don't you begin?"

The next hour was taken up with the proposals laid out by her boss and scooter man. Simon asked a ton of questions. At times he was leaning over her as he studied some of the papers she'd produced. At times she tingled as she felt him brush against her lightly. She caught his breath. It was fresh, no odour. Whenever he put his hands on the desk as he was reading over her shoulder to take his weight, Jenny wanted to stroke them. It was causing her no end of problems, but she had to remain focussed and ignore the smell of the aftershave, his animal presence, his looks, the whole bloody gamut.

And then it came to an end. Simon's phoned trilled away on his desk. He picked it up. Then he looked at his watch.

"Oh my goodness, thank you, Hannah. Yes, I'd completely forgot."

He put the phone down. "My next appointment. It's with my father, so I daren't miss it."

"Your father?"

He smiled. "He used to be a director with Trojan Engineering. He was the boss basically, but ill health forced him to pull back. He's okay now but likes to come into work from time to time. I suppose you could say it's like an honorary role. And I will be going to see him, not the other way around."

Jenny started gathering up her papers. "I'd better get on then," she said. "I wouldn't want you to get into trouble."

"Oh, I love that," he said, looking directly into her eyes. "You're concerned for me, so how about repaying me for

28

making me late?"

"Making you late?"

"You're the only reason I forgot everything about my busy schedule." He leaned forward, both elbows on the desk. "I have a confession: we could have got through all that stuff in half the time, but I didn't want it to end."

Jenny's hands began to tingle. She wanted to reach up and kiss him. He looked ready for it. But she remembered the reason she was there and shut the dream away.

"I'd better get going."

She jammed the papers back into her briefcase and reached her hand out. "Goodbye, Simon. I guess you will be in touch."

"No doubt about that," he said silkily.

As Jenny turned to walk over to the door, he came round the desk and stood in front of her. "Would you have dinner with me tonight?"

Jenny wanted to say yes, yes, yes. But she didn't; she prevaricated. "Oh, well, I need to check my diary. And I..."

"And you don't have a boyfriend."

She looked taken aback. "What? How do you know that?"

"Come on, Jenny, own up. That was just an excuse you pulled yesterday to avoid making a date with me."

She looked down at the floor and chuckled. "Am I that easy to read?"

"So you will?" His eyes lifted in expectation.

She nodded. "Yes, that would be nice."

"Do you know the George and Dragon at Houghton?"

"Yes."

"I'll pick you up. Seven o'clock?"

"You don't know where I live."

He raised his eyebrows. Jenny put her hands to her mouth.

"Oh my goodness, you don't, surely?"

He shook his head. "No I don't. So send me a text and I'll return it with an emoji." He took her arm gently and opened the door. "Please excuse me for not walking you out, but my father has his office here on this floor, and by now he will be champing at the bit. See you tonight. Oh, you won't need a taxi back to Chichester; I'll have one of our drivers take you back to your office."

Jenny walked out of Trojan Design Concepts like she was floating. She couldn't remember much about the meeting, but she didn't care. For once in her life she had met someone who she could warm to, who was pleasant and not really a motor mouth. Sue would be delighted for her.

Chapter 5

Jenny chose a simple black dress with a small diamond broach worth at least twenty pounds but looked expensive, a generous spray of Opium, a perfume she'd bought herself, and a pair of red, imitation Jimmy Choo stiletto heels, which would have cost a fortune if they'd been the real deal. But Jenny's most important and endearing attraction was her blonde hair: real, natural, and styled by her friend, Sue.

She was attractive too, and that helped.

The phone vibrated on her coffee table. She hurried over from the mirror and picked the phone up. It was a text message. *I'm here!* Smiling emoji as well.

She gave a little whoop of joy, put the phone in her handbag, checked herself over in the mirror and picked up a smart shoulder wrap she'd found in a charity shop.

Simon was standing at the front entrance to the block in which Jenny lived. He had parked in someone's private space knowing he would only be there a short while. The front door opened and Jenny appeared.

Simon whistled softly; she looked gorgeous. But he knew she would; he'd spent most of that hour with Jenny in the office that morning admiring her and taking very little notice of the marketing plan she was trying to sell him. Not very professional, he knew, but what could a man do when in the company of such a gorgeous woman?

Jenny smiled at him as she let the door close behind her.

"Hallo, Simon. You found it okay?"

"What would we do without Satnavs?"

He reached forward and kissed her lightly on the cheek. He didn't think she would be offended; it was simply a greeting. Better than an air kiss too. He turned away and pointed towards his car.

Jenny looked over at the two seater Jaguar. In the failing light she was unable to determine its colour, not that it mattered; often the car said more about the man. And this one spoke to her in spades.

She slid into the comfortable, white leather seat, fastened her seat belt, and looked at Simon as he leant forward and started the car. She had time to admire his jawline, his dark, almost wavy hair that looked completely natural, and his perfect profile.

She wondered why she hadn't switched on to all this when she first saw him at the festival. She knew why it didn't happen at the office: she was too bound up in controlling her nerves, her emotions and trying to close an important deal at the same time. If she'd known that Simon hadn't paid much attention to all that, she would never have agreed to seeing him again.

The journey to the pub at Houghton took about twenty minutes. It was a comfortable ride, and they only indulged in small talk. Simon swung into the car park and stopped. He looked at Jenny, smiled and got out of the car.

Jenny tried not to show too much leg as she eased her way out of the seat. Simon held the door open for her and made no attempt to show discretion as he watched Jenny's skirt ride up in her efforts to extricate herself tidily. It was fair game, he thought.

They walked into the pub like two people who looked comfortable in their own skins. To the onlooker, they could have been married with a couple of kids at home, a courting couple, or maybe even a married man and his mistress. That would have been more interesting and intriguing to anyone thinking along those lines.

They were shown to their table which was by a window overlooking the terrace that looked out over the South Downs. It was too dark to see anything except the moon sitting just above the hills. They ordered drinks: white wine for Jenny, sparkling water for Simon.

"I never drink when I'm driving," he told her as the waitress went off to fetch the drinks.

"Especially not when racing."

He smiled. "A friend of mine flew Harrier jump jets in the Royal Air Force. They always believed in the adage 'eight hours from bottle to throttle'. Any time I was racing, I avoided alcohol in much the same way."

"Oh, you sound too good to be true."

"What, you'd sooner have me as a boozer? No brains?"

"I think you're too clever to be like that. Risk a career because of drink."

He reached his hand over the table and laid it gently on Jenny's. She immediately felt that disarming tingle flow up her arm and interfere with her heart rate.

"Let's not start psychoanalysing each other. It might spoil things."

She cleared her throat softly. "Let's order then. Recommend anything?"

"I usually have a meat pie," he told her. "What about you?"

"Smoked salmon please."

Simon nodded over at the waitress who came and took their order.

"Can we talk about this morning?" she asked.

"Do you really want to?"

She laughed softly and shook her head. "No."

"Well, let's not. I couldn't tell you anything anyway." He shrugged. "It's out of my hands. So let's talk about each other: what we've done, what our plans are. You know — that kind of thing."

And so they began, tentatively, to probe, to inquire, to uncover each other's lives, their secrets, their plans. It was going well when suddenly there was sense of someone standing there watching them.

Simon noticed and looked up. Jenny followed his gaze. The shock and surprise on his face was clearly evident as he stood up quickly and spoke to the very attractive woman who had come up to their table.

"Anna? What a lovely surprise."

Anna offered her cheek which Simon kissed. He turned towards Jenny. "This is Jenny, a business associate. Jenny, this is Anna Duplessis, a close friend of mine."

Anna acknowledged Jenny rather condescendingly. At least, that was how it felt to Jenny. She returned the greeting. Something clicked in her brain: this was the woman she'd seen embracing Simon at the Revival when she was pulling away from the traders' car park.

"Evening, Anna. Nice to meet you." Liar, she thought. Just when I was getting on swimmingly with Simon and you have to show up and break the spell.

Anna turned to Simon; Jenny was no longer part of the conversation. "What on earth are you doing here, my darling?"

"Jenny was at the office this morning discussing a contract. This is a way of thanking her for her hard work. You know the drill," he added.

She leaned in very close. "I know exactly what you mean, my darling." She whispered softly in his ear; soft enough so Jenny couldn't hear. "You don't have to sleep with them as well."

She straightened. "Are we still okay for Wednesday evening? You're not dumping me just yet, are you?"

He laughed with a little constraint. "No fear of that, Anna. Yes, I'll see you on Wednesday."

Anna looked at Jenny. "Enjoy your evening." She wrinkled her nose a little and made a pointing motion with her forefinger. "Don't let it get out of hand though." She blew a kiss at Simon and walked away into the interior of the bar.

Simon watched until she was no longer in sight, then sat down.

"Sorry about that," he said. "An old friend of mine."

Jenny could tell he was lying. Well, maybe not lying, but more like a man who has been caught with his pants down. Not that it mattered; she had no claim on him, but the evening had crumbled, and there was no way to recapture it.

"I think I would like to go now, Simon. Please."

He was cute enough to recognise Jenny's crushing disappointment at Anna's unexpected appearance. He knew Jenny had no claim on him, other than she was his dinner partner for the evening. He had hoped it would have been for the night, but that was now blown out of the water.

Jenny stood up and excused herself. "I'm going to the loo," she said.

When she got in there, she went into a cubicle, sat down, had a sprinkle, and sat there with her head in her hands cursing Anna Duplessis.

The spell had been broken. It was obvious the woman

35

was probably one of many that Simon had slept with. No doubt he expected the same would happen tonight. Jenny had to admit she may not have offered any resistance, but now, sleeping with Simon was the last thing she wanted.

She went back to the table. Simon was just paying the bill. He waited for her to pick up her handbag and they walked out of the pub into the night.

Chapter 6

Jenny kicked off her shoes and poured herself a glass of wine, picked up the remote and aimed it at the TV. She took a mouthful of the wine; put the glass down on the work surface and wandered through to the bedroom as her phone vibrated in her handbag. She sat on the bed and took her phone out. It was a text message from Simon.

Thank you for tonight. Simon. xx

No emoji? She sniffed and tossed the phone on the bed, undressed, and slipped her PJs on. She felt a little more relaxed now. The irritation and frustration at that woman's appearance was gradually melting away. Jenny knew she shouldn't feel annoyed just because one of Simon's girlfriends had stopped to say hello. But it was that little bit in the middle: the quiet whispering in his ear. Bloody cheek, she thought. And in front of her too!

She went through to the front room, dimmed the lights, and found a soppy romance on Netflix. Ten minutes later she was fast asleep on the couch while some other woman was getting lucky on the TV.

Jenny woke suddenly, startled, not sure where she was for a moment. Her phone had beeped somewhere announcing a message. It took her a while to find it, searching frantically on the couch before she realised it was still on the bed. She dashed through and scooped up the phone. It was Simon again.

You didn't answer. Are you OK? xx

No emoji again? *Thank you, yes. I was asleep.*

Good. Hope to see you soon. Sweet dreams. xx

She turned the phone off, went back into the lounge and turned the TV off. Then she went back to bed hoping that if she was going to have sweet dreams they would be about Simon and not that Anna depressing, whatever her name was. She offered up a little prayer before turning her light off and fell asleep wondering if her she had managed to sell the marketing idea to Simon.

***

The following morning, Jenny breezed into work, actually acknowledged the security guy in the front entrance and took the lift up to KJ Marketing. She felt optimistic for some reason. Probably the fact that Simon had messaged her twice. He seemed concerned that she hadn't replied to his first text message. She smiled at that thought; it was something like having him on a lead. No, not Simon she thought, not with Anna depressing around.

She waved at the early birds in the office. One of the girls held up a coffee for her. It was her turn that week for coffee; Jenny's would come in a couple of weeks according to the rota. She liked that idea. Well ordered. Friendly. Just how KJ would want it.

She dropped into the chair at her desk behind the cubicle wall that defined her small space and booted up her computer. First task was to check her face in the small mirror she kept in her handbag, touch up the lip gloss, then open up her emails.

My office. Soon as you can. KJ

She slumped in the chair. Bloody woman, why can't she wait? She sighed, took a swig of coffee, and heaved herself out of the chair. She raised her eyebrows and grimaced as she walked past the coffee girl. That was returned with a good luck crossing of the fingers.

Jenny tapped on the door and pushed it open.

"Good morning, KJ. You wanted to see me?"

KJ pointed at the chair but said nothing, just kept her eyes on the computer screen. Finally she sighed, blew out her cheeks and settled back in her chair.

"How did you get on?"

Jenny drew in a deep breath as quietly as she could before answering. "I thought I got on okay. "

"Just 'okay'?"

"Well, we seemed to bond, if that's the right word. It took me best part of an hour to go through the proposals. Mister Daines was very attentive of course, but there wasn't much he could say. I think he liked them though."

"And?"

Jenny shrugged. "Well, that was it. He had to cut short the meeting because he had an appointment with his father."

KJ kept her eyes fixed on Jenny with a look on her face that made Jenny think she wanted more. But there was no more to give; that was it.

"And what about last night?"

"Last night?"

"You had dinner with Mister Baines."

That shook Jenny. "How did you know Simon, er, Mister Baines had asked me out to dinner."

KJ allowed a sly grin to escape across her mouth. "As they say: a little bird told me."

Bloody Anna depressing thought Jenny.

"And did you sleep with Mister Daines."

Jenny's mouth fell wide open in shock. "No I did not," she said indignantly. "I don't sleep with clients just to get a sale."

KJ sniffed. "Well perhaps you should." Jenny was about to say something but her boss held up her hand.

"I'm going over to Trojan later today."

For a moment, Jenny's heart lifted, thinking she was going to be asked to go with her. It had to be about the contract.

"I will be taking Miranda," KJ went on. "You can drop on to anything else that needs your attention." She fixed a grin on her face that Jenny wanted to wipe off with a massive slap. Miranda was the senior girl at KJ Marketing, if that was the right word. Well, she'd been there longer than anyone else. And she did know her stuff; Jenny had to admit that much.

"Thank you, KJ. Is there anything else?"

"No, not for you."

The meeting was over; Jenny had been dismissed. And as she walked out of KJ's office she felt that her days at KJ marketing were coming to an end. If they'd ever really started.

The morning dragged by for Jenny, but as soon as the hand hit one o'clock, she was out of there and round to Sue's hairdressing salon as quick as she could. They often shared their lunchbreaks. Sometimes Sue would still be with a customer, but generally they managed best part of an hour. Jenny's lunchbreak was flexible. That was the one good thing about KJ: she never complained about extended breaks so long as the hours were put in during the day and the work completed.

Once they had their latte coffees and egg salad in front of them, Jenny opened up about her meeting with Simon and the interruption by Anna Duplessis that killed the evening stone dead for her.

"Why? She only wanted to say hello," Sue pointed out.

"It was the little bloody tête a tête in his ear that pissed me off. I could have killed her."

"Who was she?"

"Simon told me her name was Anna Duplessis. I think of her as Anna depressing."

Sue laughed. "Well, she really got to you then. What did she look like?"

"Fucking gorgeous really, I have to admit." She scooped up a mouthful of salad. "Simon practically melted when she spoke to him." A piece of lettuce hung out from her mouth. Sue reached over the table and flicked it off with her finger.

"He took you home though. Didn't send you back in a taxi?"

Jenny chuckled. "That would have been really depressing." She shook her head. "No, I cut the evening short; the magic just seemed to go out of it."

"Are you going to see him again?"

Another mouthful of salad went in. "I doubt it." She told Sue about the meeting with KJ. "It looks like I'm out. She'll probably let me go soon. Make up some pretext about costs, need to cut staff. The usual dribble." She leaned forward. "You know, she even implied that I should have slept with Simon to secure the sale."

Sue's mouth opened wide. "Really? You wouldn't have done that, would you?"

Jenny looked a little sheepish. "I had hoped," she said. "But it had nothing to do with the contract."

Her phone buzzed on the table. She picked it up and looked at the name of the caller. It was KJ.

"Hello, KJ."

"What are you doing?"

"I'm at lunch."

"Well get yourself back here quick as you can. I want you to come with me to Trojan."

"But I thought you were taking Miranda."

"Didn't I just tell you that you're coming with me?"

"Yes, sorry, KJ. I'll be back as soon as I can."

The phone call was disconnected. Jenny put her phone down and stared at Sue. "Bugger, she wants me to go with her to Trojan's."

Sue grabbed her hand. "So you're still in?"

"Guess so. Unless Miranda fell down and broke her leg." She drained her cup. "I'd better go," she said. "Can't keep KJ waiting."

"Nor Simon," Sue said with a huge smile and her eyebrows raised in a triumphant expression.

***

The ride out to Trojan's was difficult for Jenny. She had a lot of questions buzzing around in her brain but didn't want to ask too much. KJ could be an awkward woman to talk to. But she wanted to know why Miranda had been dropped. So she asked.

"It's quite simple," KJ answered as she swept past a dawdling motorist. "Mister Daines specifically asked for you." She risked a quick glance at Jenny. "Perhaps you did sleep with him but was afraid to tell me."

Jenny didn't answer; she thought it would be something of a tease to leave her boss wondering.

KJ turned into a visitors parking bay and turned off the engine. As Jenny unbuckled her seat belt, KJ touched her lightly on the arm.

"Leave the talking to me," she said.

Jenny muttered an acknowledgement and got out of the car. She opened the rear door and lifted her briefcase from the passenger seat and joined her boss.

The receptionist asked them to wait. Jenny's mind went back to the previous day and wondered if it would be Simon who would come down for them. But she was to be disappointed; a young girl, no more than about eighteen or nineteen years of age stepped out of the lift and came over, a big smile breaking out on her face as she said hello to them.

"Good afternoon, Ms Johnson. And Miss Paige, yes?"

Jenny smiled. "Miss Paige is fine." KJ said nothing, just dipped her head a little at the girl and barely touched her fingers as an apology for a handshake.

"I'm Sarah. If you put these visitors' passes on, I'll take you up to Mister Daines."

They followed Sarah into the lift and on the top floor they followed her out to a fine looking, glass fronted conference room with a magnificent view over the South Downs. Sarah pointed to the chairs.

"I'll tell Mister Daines you're here."

"It's okay, Sarah. Beat you to it!"

They all looked round as Simon strode into the conference room. He shook hands with KJ and Jenny, thanked Sarah and asked her to bring coffee or tea or whatever the ladies wanted. KJ said water was sufficient. Jenny wanted a double brandy but settled for water.

She couldn't get her eyes of Simon. She didn't want to either. She was looking for something in his face that might acknowledge their evening together and the fact that she had brought it to an end rather abruptly, and the fact that he had asked for her to attend the meeting. But there was nothing; just the look of a professional, a businessman about to discuss company matters with two important clients.

Sarah put a jug of water and two glasses in front of them. Simon waved his away. Sarah then left the conference room and disappeared. This was the moment when KJ decided to open her briefcase and pull out some documentation. Simon stopped her.

"Ms. Johnson. Before we discuss the proposals Miss Paige put before us yesterday, I need to put something to you."

Jenny wondered if he'd even bothered to look at the proposals. She shut that away and listened to what he had to say.

"I've spoken with my brother, Harry, and we have decided, subject to your understanding, that if we reached an agreement on your proposals, we would like KJ Marketing to work here at Trojan Design Concepts. We have a suitable office available."

That threw KJ for a moment. But she gathered herself together and immediately saw the benefits of working directly inside the business: almost like a contractor with a foot in the door. It would allow KJ Marketing to benefit from the powerful reach it had into the high tech world of cutting edge technology and bring KJ Marketing's brand to the forefront of that lucrative market.

Jenny thought how lovely it would be to see Simon every day, spend time with him going over different aspects of Trojan's business and maybe even getting a few more romantic dinners in, so long as they were miles away from Anna depressing.

She was still musing over the idyllic rather than the object of working here when KJ asked about the finer detail, and how would they arrive at an agreement that protected KJ Marketing's role in Trojan's establishment.

"It's dead simple, Ms Johnson. Our lawyers will draw up a straightforward contract that protects KJ Marketing's proprietary rights. While you are working here, you would be basically a free entity with no interference from Trojan, and vice versa." He looked over at Jenny. "What do you say, Miss Paige?"

"If I'm to be working here, then please call me Jenny."

He smiled and winked at her. KJ fidgeted. Jenny almost wilted. "Jenny it is then." He stood up, gathered up some papers that were in front of him. "Perhaps you could start tomorrow? HR will take care of the initial steps, but it will just be a case of turning up, getting your feet under the table and learn a little about what we do here while we are waiting for the lawyers to run off an agreement."

Jenny was cock-a-hoop but trying hard not to show it. KJ acted a little differently.

"Mister Daines, we haven't talked about our marketing proposals."

Simon flashed that smile at her. "I did it last night with my brother. Had nothing else important to do as a result of my evening plans being changed." He looked at Jenny. It was all she could do to hide the blush that was creeping up round her neck. "Everything is fine." He straightened up. The meeting was over. "Now, ladies, I'll get Sarah to escort you off the premises and will expect to see you very soon."

Five minutes later they were sitting in KJ's car. KJ was sitting in stunned silence. Jenny was feeling warm all over. Particularly when she realised that Simon had asked for her and invited her to start working with him the following day. It was almost too much for her to take.

KJ started the car. "I didn't expect that, Jenny. You obviously didn't need to sleep with him." She turned and looked at Jenny. "Did you?"

Jenny felt smug. "No, KJ, I promise. It had to be my business acumen and charm that swung it."

KJ actually laughed. "Well, you know what to do if you want to end up as CEO of Trojan Design Concepts." She pulled out of the visitors parking bay. "Sleep with the boss!"

Chapter 7

Simon watched KJ's car pull away from the parking area and accelerate out on to the main road. There was little traffic, which gave him a clear view until the car disappeared from sight. He sighed and turned away, only to see his brother Harry standing there watching him.

"Don't get involved, bro," Harry said. "Strictly business, don't forget."

Simon smiled. "You think I'm going too quick?"

"Well, three days and you're practically sleeping with her."

Simon put his arm around Harry's shoulder. "I can usually crack them in less than a couple of hours." He glanced back at the window. "This one is different though," he muttered thoughtfully. "It could take a little longer."

They started walking towards Simon's office.

"That serious?"

Simon nudged his brother away. "Of course not. Just takes more planning, that's all. But Jenny has class, and I don't want to look at her as a conquest. I really like her."

"So the idea of her working here on site? Did you put that to her as part of your plan?"

Simon pushed open the door to his office. "Not straight away," he admitted. "But the longer she sat there, the more I wanted to keep her here."

"You be careful, Simon," Harry warned him. "She isn't a chattel for you to do what you want with."

The two of them walked through. Harry sat down while Simon went to a cupboard and pulled a bottle of single malt whisky out.

"I'm not going to do that to her," he said as he held the bottle up. "Drink, Harry?"

"What's this for? A celebration?"

Simon didn't answer, just poured a short measure into each glass. He gave one to his brother and held his forward. As they touched glasses, Simon winked.

"I didn't have to sell the idea to Jenny; it was the boss, KJ — Ms. Johnson." He downed his whisky and put the glass on the desk. "I know how to handle them, Harry, you know I do."

"You bombed out last night though."

Simon flopped down into his chair. "Yeah, bloody Anna showed up. Things were going really well." He held his hand out, palm uppermost. "I had her eating out of my hand. I thought it would go on all night."

Harry chuckled at his brother's arrogance. "She'll bite you in the bum one day, bro. Mark my words." He drained his glass and stood up. "I have to go; got work to do."

Simon watched his brother leave the office, his mind on the prospect of beginning to work *with* KJ Marketing and to work *on* Jenny. He knew it had to be unlike all his other conquests. This girl was different, he thought. And special.

His phone buzzed at him. He picked it up and saw the message icon highlighted. It was Jenny.

Have to delay my start until next week. KJ's orders. I'll call you tomorrow. Jenny xx.

He turned the phone off. Bollocks, he thought to himself; now it's going to take a little longer.

***

"Well done, you," Sue chimed as she held up her glass to Jenny. "Just like that. Amazing."

Jenny affected a coy pose. "It was nothing," she said.

48

"He was swept away by my good looks and my charm."

Sue stopped her. "Whoa, whoa. I thought it was your business skills, your brilliant mind putting so much detail into the marketing project."

Jenny laughed. "No, that was scooter man."

Sue lowered her glass. "And how is he getting on?"

Jenny wrinkled her nose. "I should imagine he's well pissed off by now, particularly when he finds out I've pulled the rug from under his feet." She stared dreamily up towards the ceiling. "Just imagine: I'll be rubbing shoulders with the hi-tech world of innovative design and technology, while he'll be stuck listening to KJ banging on about work ethic and all that."

"And you'll be banging Simon."

Jenny grinned, her eyes lighting up. "That too."

"What's he like close up?"

Jenny let her shoulders sag a little as she pictured Simon in her mind. "He's gorgeous, Sue. Good company. Attentive. When we were discussing the marketing proposals, it felt like he was all over me, but in a different way. It was as though he was more interested in me than the plan."

"And you were giving off oodles of pheromones, just like a predatory female."

Jenny snorted. "You don't need to be predatory: just horny."

Sue leaned back in the chair, twiddling her glass on the table. "It's a wonder you didn't hook up on the bloody desk." She stood up. "Want another?"

Jenny nodded and watched her friend go up to the bar. She liked Sue enormously: loved her like a sister. She only wished she could help sell her books. Jenny knew it took money and marketing to succeed in the book world. You could sell good and bad books with good marketing, and she knew Sue couldn't afford all that. She imagined, hoped really, that one day she would be in a position to offer her own marketing expertise in helping Sue to sell her books.

Sue came back with the drinks. "How long before you bed him?" she asked, a twinkle in her eye."

Jenny took a sip of the cocktail. "Well, the thing is — do I play him, or do I just drag him into bed?"

"Where's the fun in that?" Sue asked. "He'll shag you at the drop of a hat because you're gorgeous and fuckable. He knows that. You know that." She leaned forward and lowered her voice, whispering conspiratorially. "You want him begging. Bring him to his knees, salivating."

Jenny laughed and put her hand on Sue's." "Slow down, girl. I don't plan to see him until next week. Although he might respond to a bog standard text message. You know: looking forward to working with you etc. etc."

"Then don't let the lustre die: keep the gilt on the gingerbread by staying silent all week. He'll be champing on the bit by then."

Jenny lifted her glass and they toasted each other. "To legs and books, may they both be opened frequently!"

They roared with laughter and touched their glasses together in a silent toast.

***

Three days later, Anna Duplessis phoned KJ.

"Morning, Kathleen, how are you this morning? Not hungover I hope."

Kathleen raised her eyebrows, remembering the amount of champagne the two of them had put away the previous evening.

"I'm a little fragile, Anna, but I'll hibernate until lunchtime."

Anna had invited KJ out to dinner unexpectedly. KJ was always alert to business opportunities, and a dinner invitation from someone important to Cobalt Racing was a chance to cement a relationship and pry open a door to marketing opportunities.

KJ learned the previous evening that Anna was involved in a new subdivision of Cobalt known as Cobalt E. The Company were venturing into Electric car racing and planned the get involved in Formula E once they had built, tested, and trialled a new Concept car.

Anna was a software programmer, a shareholder at Cobalt, and held a high ranking role in the new division. Cobalt were talking to Trojan about a merger with Trojan's fledgling racing department, and Anna hinted at KJ Marketing getting involved if the Companies started talking serious business.

"I was delighted to hear about your contract with Trojan," Anna said down the phone. "You could become a fixture with them, you know. The girl, Jenny. Is it Jenny?"

"Yes. But I thought you knew that. You told me you'd seen her with Mister Daines at the pub earlier this week."

"You're right, but she was a stranger to me. But I am right, aren't I? It is Jenny who will be working with Simon — Mister Daines."

"For now, yes. We'll see."

"Oh I'm sure she will do well. Simon can be very accommodating you know: in more ways than one."

KJ wasn't daft; she knew what Anna was implying. "I'm sure Jenny has the sense to know that you cannot mix business with pleasure."

"Of course. But Kathleen, I didn't call you to talk about your contract with Trojan: that's your business. No, I thought that you might like to come over to Cobalt and have a chat. Nothing other than getting to know each other. Now that you've stepped into the high tech world over here at Goodwood, I thought perhaps you could run your eye over our idea of Cobalt E, have a think, see if there is any way we might improve our image. We are supposed to do that by winning races, but there is always a public perception about the character of a company."

"I know exactly what you mean, Anna. And I would be delighted to come over to Cobalt. Just give me a time and date and I'll pencil it into my diary."

Anna gave KJ a couple of dates. "Oh, and KJ, could we keep this between ourselves for now? Until after you've been to Cobalt."

"Of course, Anna. No problem."

"Good. I'll see you later then. Just text me the date you want and I'll get Cobalt to confirm it. Bye for now."

KJ put the phone down, a warm feeling brushing away any effects from their drinking the previous evening.

Anna put the phone down and smiled. It was more of a smile of satisfaction. Now she was closer to KJ Marketing, the closer she would be to Simon and Jenny: his bit on the side.

Chapter 8

Jenny was a lot happier now she knew she would be spending less time in KJ's company, and more time with Simon. She had even managed to smile and say good morning to the security guy, such was her lifted spirits, no longer experiencing the mood drop as she walked to the lift.

She'd been working on the Trojan project for a short while, acknowledging the good wishes from her colleagues, each one conveying the unspoken message, '*you jammy sod'*, when scooter man came up to her desk. She looked up.

"Hello, Jack. You back now?"

"Hi, Jenny. Yes, back, and raring to go."

"Are you okay? No damage?"

"You mean to my ego, or my body?"

She felt her colour come flooding into her cheeks. "Yes, I'm sorry about the contract, Jack. I didn't expect it, I promise you."

He looked back round the office and then at Jenny, a conspiratorial look on his face. "Don't you worry about that. I have to admit I was quite relieved when KJ broke the news to me."

A frown rippled across Jenny's forehead. "Really? Why?"

He pulled an empty office chair over to the desk and sat down beside her. "While I was preparing the pitch, I spent a little time over at Trojan. I have to say that I never felt comfortable there. I was only ever there for about an hour or two, but it was always as if I was an interloper."

Jenny chuckled. "Well, you were, weren't you?"

He tapped her playfully on the arm. "Sez you."

"You think I should be worried?"

He shook his head. "No, it will be different for you; you're a woman."

Jenny shook her head. "Oh come on, Jack. I'll be there in a professional capacity, doing a job. It's what we do here," she pointed out, sweeping her hand across her desk.

"Yes, but you're not a Trojan. Oh, that's how they like to refer to each other."

Jenny laughed. "But maybe I'll be like Helen of Troy's Trojan: in the company secretly, doing my best to bring it down."

Jack laughed at that. "Some feat, that would be. Trojan are huge, remember that."

"Any other advice, Jack?" she asked.

"No, but I did hear that Cobalt Racing have been taking a covert interest in KJ Marketing. Make of that what you will."

"Should I be worried?"

"You might need to be careful if you come into contact with Anna Duplessis. A good software engineer by all accounts. She holds a lot of influence in their offshoot Electric race car division. And she is practically engaged to Simon Daines. Imagine a merger between those two."

Jenny pulled a face. "Physical?"

He pursed his lips. "Could be. But just remember that if Simon Daines shows too much interest in you, Miss Duplessis could make life difficult."

"But only if I show too much of an interest in Simon Daines," she said. "And I'm not likely to." She crossed her fingers tightly beneath the desk. "Am I?"

He stood up, rubbed his back, and groaned a little.

"Bloody scooter."

"Do you still plan on using it, Jack? Sounds too dangerous to me."

He looked down at her and fixed a knowing grin on his face. "No more than working for Trojan and crossing swords with Helen of Troy."

Jenny watched him walk away and felt a little happier after talking with him. Not because of what he had to say about Trojan, but that he held no grudge against her for being given the job he should have had.

She went back to her computer and put Jack, Trojan, and Anna Duplessis to the back of her mind. Well, she tried to, but images of Simon and Anna coupling kept popping into her head. She had to remind herself that she had no claim on Simon, and if she was to be true to her word, she would treat her new role at Trojan's as professionally as she could.

***

Over at Trojan Design Concepts, Simon's secretary, Hannah, was putting the finishing touches to the timetable for a gala dinner to be held a few weeks later. It was a way of acknowledging the part played by most of the employees in securing a major contract with Stark Aviation who had announced a government funded grant to design and manufacture a drone concept for use in the country's defence programme.

Simon was over at the design department when his phone buzzed in his pocket. He checked the screen to see his father's name next to a smiling emoji. That meant his father had just arrived in his office and would like a few minutes of his time. When he got back, his father was there talking to Hannah.

"Morning, Simon. Hannah's been telling me about the dinner. Looks good."

"Morning, Dad. It's always nice to thank everyone for their hard work."

Hannah got up from her desk. "I'll leave you two to talk," she said as she closed down her computer and picked up a folder. "I've emailed the details to you, Mister Simon. Anything you need to know..."

"Thank you, Hannah."

He waited until she had left the room and then sat down opposite his father. "Can I get you a coffee, Dad?"

His father shook his head. "No thank you, Simon. One thing Trojan cannot do is make decent coffee."

"Not enough brandy in it for you?" Simon joked.

His father ignored the cryptic comment. "I've been looking at this idea of yours to have a marketing company here at Trojan."

"It isn't the whole company, Dad. Just one rep from KJ Marketing."

"A bit unusual though, don't you think?"

"It isn't rocket science, Dad. We had a spare room; it makes it easier to have them on site where we can deal with any issues or problems rather than texting or emails. Harry will be overseeing the whole project. He'll enjoy that; KJ have supplied us with a very attractive rep."

His father opened his mouth and lifted his chin. "Oh, I get it: not enough skirt on site for you, eh?"

"Who says it's a woman?"

"Well, is it?"

Simon nodded quickly and shrugged. "As you say, Dad."

"I think I know you better than you know yourself."

Simon grinned at that. His father went on. "By the way, did you know that Anna is toying with the idea of using KJ Marketing?"

"I heard a whisper, Dad. Why do you ask?"

"Well, I believe you and Anna are planning to announce your engagement soon, but I did wonder if Anna had an ulterior motive."

Simon frowned. "How so?"

"It's just that she has suddenly developed an interest in KJ Marketing without even knowing how successful they are, what's involved, and why so soon after you've taken them on as well?"

"You're seeing spooks, Dad. Anna is perfectly entitled to run her business the way she sees fit. I'm sure she will have put a great deal of thought into it. Don't let it worry you."

His father tipped his head a little to one side. "Okay, Simon, I'll wind my neck in. It's your —"

"My funeral, Dad?" he interrupted.

His father laughed. "No, of course not, so let's change the subject and talk about the Stark contract."

Simon nodded. "Much better idea, Dad. Let's do that, and no mention of my tangled love life," he added with a grin. "And by the way— Anna and I are not engaged. Nor are we planning to announce an engagement."

***

KJ came storming into the office.

"Jack, Jenny! My office. Now if you please."

Jenny looked across at Jack and raised her eyebrows. Jack lifted his hands and shrugged his shoulders. They both gathered up a notepad and pen and walked over to KJ's door which she had left open.

KJ was busy booting up her computer as the two of them sat down. She looked at them both.

"Right, bit of business. Jenny, you start over at Trojan on Monday, right?"

You know I bloody do, Jenny thought to herself. "Yes, KJ. Monday."

"Jack, I'm sorry I took you off the Trojan contract, but I didn't know when you might recover from your riding accident."

That's a smart way of describing it, Jenny thought. Must be the marketing skill she has.

"Yes, KJ," Jack answered. "Fully recovered."

"Right, now what we are about to discuss must not leave this room. Are we clear on that?" They both nodded. "Good. Now, Anna Duplessis has approached me, in the utmost confidentiality, about KJ Marketing filling a role in Cobalt Racing.

Both Jenny and Jack raised their eyebrows and looked at each other.

"Well, that's good news," Jenny offered. "Two important companies in less than a week."

KJ glared at her. "It's bullshit," she said harshly. "Miss Duplessis no more wants our business than I want to fly to the moon. She's angling for something, but I can't put my finger on it. I will though."

"So why are you telling us this, KJ?" Jenny asked.

"Because you will be my eyes and ears at Trojan, and Jack." She turned to him. "I want you to look at anything I bring back from Cobalt and find what it is she wants."

"Perhaps she really is just looking to do business with us," Jack put in. "It wouldn't be the first time we've picked up other work from a current project."

58

KJ nodded. "Yes, you're right, Jack, but this one is too convenient. It's as though she's jumping on the bandwagon because Trojan have taken us on."

"Well, they are supposed to be jumping into bed together soon, so I hear."

KJ almost snarled. "Trojan are too big. They would suck Cobalt in and blow them out in bubbles." She shook her head and looked quite stern. "No, she's looking for an angle: something to use as pressure on Trojan. Or more likely, Simon Daines. And if, whatever she is planning collapses, the fall out could be disastrous for us. We'd be out on our ear with our reputation in tatters."

"So let me understand this, KJ. What do you expect us to do?"

"Jack will filter out all the noise while you, Jenny, will report anything and everything you get from Simon Daines. And if it's pillow talk, so much the better."

***

Jenny pulled up in a visitors' parking bay at Trojan Design Concepts and locked her ageing KIA Picanto. There was a larger car park for employees, but the security guy at the front entrance had told her where to park. She carried her laptop in one bag and a sheaf of paperwork in another hoping it wouldn't be too long before she found a home for them.

The receptionist handed Jenny a visitor's tag and asked her to wait until someone came down to fetch her. In the end it was someone she hadn't seen before. She had hoped it would have been Simon. The young woman shook her hand.

"Good morning, Miss Paige, I'm Hannah, Mister Simon's secretary. You must remember to address him like that, Mister Harry too; they prefer it that way." She gave Jenny a knowing look. "It retains the status quo and just helps us all to know where we are in the pyramid." She affected a conspiratorial aside. "But don't tell them I said that."

Jenny wasn't taken to a plush office on the top floor with a beautiful view over the South Downs. Instead she was taken to a small room on the ground floor overlooking a yard, which looked like it was used to dump stuff that was destined for the rubbish tip.

"Make yourself at home," Hannah told her. "There's a phone there. My number is four. Just press it and that will put you through to me. That's it. There's a drinks machine in the front lobby. If you need anything, just give me a shout. Someone will be down to see you soon. Good luck!"

And with that she was gone. Nothing about Mister Simon or Mister Harry, just the bare room, it's grey walls offering no comfort and no welcome. All there was in that room was a table, an office chair, a filing cabinet, a phone, and a computer terminal.

She dropped her bag and laptop on the desk and sat in the chair, flummoxed. So much for the high tech world of Trojan Design Concepts, she thought. I'd be better off in a bloody charity shop.

Chapter 9

Jenny wandered out into the front lobby and found the drinks machine. She ignored the cold drinks and bought a coffee. Then she spun slowly, taking in the surroundings, stopping to look at the glossy, etched profile of Trojan Design Concepts fixed front and centre behind the reception desk, taking in the ambience, reflecting on the peacefulness of the place. It was warm and inviting, nothing like the scattered clutter of KJ Marketing's domain. She approached the reception desk, a smile already on her face.

"Hi, can you tell me where the toilets are please?

The receptionist looked over to a screen fixed in one corner. "Behind the screen. We prefer them hidden from view."

Jenny thanked her. "Do you get much movement through here?" She looked at the young girl's name tag. "Brenda?"

"It varies. Some days we're busy, others not. Why do you ask?"

"Oh, sorry. I'm Jenny Paige. I'm with KJ Marketing."

Brenda looked at something beneath the counter. "Oh, yes; I can see you there."

"Oh good, now I feel I belong," she said brightly. "It's my first day and I need to start getting a feel for the place. You know, learn a little more about the company, the practical attributes, the people, it's…" she fumbled for a word. "Nuance."

The phone rang. Brenda picked it up. Jenny thought it best to leave the girl and get back to her rabbit hutch and pretend she was a fully paid up employee in the world of high end technology. Well, try anyway.

She finished her coffee and was giving some thought about what to do next, when there was a sudden rattling on the door. It flew open.

"Morning, Jenny." It was Simon.

Jenny beamed. "Oh my god, Simon. I thought I wasn't going to see anyone."

He bent towards her and brushed his cheek against hers. She felt that warm tingle again. Just his brief touch and seeing him there was all it needed.

"I'm sorry I wasn't here to meet you when you arrived. Had an early meeting with the board. You know how it is."

No, Jenny thought, I've no idea; it's a different world where I come from. But it didn't matter; he was here.

Simon looked around the dismal room. "Sorry about the room. Pretty grim, eh?" He perched himself on the corner of her desk. "You definitely need another chair. And something to brighten the room."

"I can deal with that," she said. "But I would like a kind of introduction to Trojan. A tour round the place would be nice. Get the feel of it. I want to learn as much as I can to help with the marketing."

Simon nodded. "I'll arrange for someone to take you round. I would do it myself, but I have several meetings lined up."

He slid off the desk and stood in front of her. From her sitting position, Jenny felt quite diminutive. But she liked looking up at him.

"I'll get Hannah to take you along to HR so you can be inducted properly, and then we'll provide the grand tour." He went to the door. "Oh, one other thing."

"What's that?"

"Will you have dinner with me tonight?"

＊

Jenny sat with a glass of white wine in her hand, thinking about the day, the evening, and the sheer satisfaction of being in Simon's company. She wasn't sure where she was; Simon had picked her up from home. He wasn't driving but had used a taxi. The driver took them out into the countryside somewhere, she didn't know where, and stopped at what looked like a coach house just inside the entrance to a private estate.

The day at Trojan's had turned out better than she had expected. Once she'd been inducted into the firm, she was taken round the site, the design office, the manufacturing department (still called the factory), and met a lot of nice, friendly people.

After lunch she was given a portfolio containing ideas of how and where Trojan wanted to go, and a password given her low grade access to some of Trojan's planned projects. At the end of the day, Jenny felt a lot happier than she did at the beginning. And as she drove home, she had the happy prospect of dinner with Simon to look forward to.

"Who do I work for, Simon?" she asked, her voice softened by the effects of the gorgeous meal and the expensive wine.

Simon sat with his chin resting in his hands, just looking at her, watching her, enjoying what he was seeing.

"Me I guess."

She giggled. "You don't mean that, do you?"

He lifted his shoulders in the smallest of shrugs. "OK, KJ Marketing. You're just attached to us, to Trojan, and to me."

"I like the sound of the last bit," she said, her eyes brightening.

"It could happen, Jenny." He leaned forward. "If you play your cards right."

She breathed in deeply and let her breath out in an almost a dreamy sigh. "And I suppose I hold the Ace card. Am I Right?"

He picked up his glass and touched Jenny's. "Well, that's one way of putting it."

He finished his drink and looked at his watch. "Time, I think Jenny, to bring this evening to a close. As much as I hate to say it: we have work tomorrow."

It was true; they both had jobs to do, although she knew Simon was not as tied to the clock as she was. She doubted he would ever take advantage of his position in the Company though.

She finished her drink and excused herself. Simon paid the bill, asked the waitress to call a taxi and waited in the entrance foyer. When she appeared, he thought he noticed her lips looked fresher than when she left the table. He knew what he wanted to do but needed to tread carefully and not to rush it.

She smiled at him and took his offered arm, once again enjoying the touch and feel. When they arrived at Jenny's house, Simon asked the driver to wait. He followed Jenny up to her small flat, and as she opened the door, he pulled her round and kissed her. Jenny felt a rush of something in her body and she almost fainted at Simon's embrace.

He let her go. "Goodnight, Jenny."

She didn't want it to stop there; she wanted him to stay. But there was a time and a place for everything, and although she was holding the Ace, Simon was playing it carefully. She respected him for that.

"Good night, Simon," she answered huskily. "Thank you for a lovely evening."

She closed the door and leaned back on it, listening to the sound of his footsteps disappearing down the stairs. Then she bolted the door, dropped her bag on the small table, kicked of her imitation Jimmy Choos and made her way to bed.

Chapter 10

The week flew by for Jenny. She saw Simon from time to time, but most of her time was spent with his brother, Harry. Although Jenny had been advised about the correct way to address the two brothers, Harry told her it was a load of balls and she could call him Harry whenever she liked.

He was extremely helpful when it came to preparing campaigns, seemed to know a great deal about promotion and marketing and allowed Jenny to have her head when discussing ideas.

She began to warm to Harry. She liked his manner, his ironic humour, and the way he dealt with problems that threatened Jenny's grasp on Trojan's work ethic. And she was tickled pink when he asked her if she would have dinner with him some time over the weekend.

"Saturday or Sunday, whatever suits you."

It took Jenny a few moments to realise that the invitation could mean missing out on seeing Simon, but at the same time she felt it would be rude to turn Harry down simply because she hoped Simon might call. Which he hadn't, so she accepted Harry's offer.

"Yes, Harry, I would like that very much. Where to?"

She shrugged. "Your choice," she said.

He clenched his lips together. "Good. Saturday. You live in Chichester, so why don't we have a stroll round town in the evening, a bit of a pub crawl and then drop in to an Indian, or a Chinese?"

"Chinese sounds good. Do you know where I live?"

He nodded. "Of course; it's on file. I'll be at your door at seven o'clock sharp. Looking forward to it."

And with that he stepped out of Jenny's little room, closing the door behind him.

Jenny continued to stare at the door, half expecting Harry to come back in and say something to her. But she sat there staring — hoping?

She shook her head suddenly, clearing her mind of the irrational thoughts that were trundling through her head, and got back to the task of making her new job at Trojan a success.

***

At seven o'clock sharp, the doorbell sounded. Jenny hurried over to the door release button, not even bothering to speak through the voice mike and ask who it was and pressed the button. Then she opened her door and leaned out into the hallway, listening to the sounds of his footsteps bounding up the stairs.

Harry appeared with a big smile on his face and a bunch of flowers in his hand.

"Evening, Jenny." He kissed her on the cheek and offered her the flowers. "You okay with these?"

She took the bouquet from him and ushered him in, closing the door behind her. "Thank you, Harry, they're lovely. I'd better put them in water."

Jenny didn't have anything to put the flowers in, never having been a flower person. But she wasn't going to let them die of thirst, so she filled the washing up bowl with water and laid the bunch so that the stems were in the water.

"I'll find something suitable later."

Harry began looking round the room, glancing at this and that. He picked up a framed photograph. "Mum and dad?" he asked.

"Yes. It was taken at Brighton some years ago."

Harry noticed a slight change in the tremor of her voice almost wistful. "Still part of your life?"

"Sort of. My father died just before my mum went into care. She has Alzheimer's and is like a cabbage."

"I'm sorry to hear that. Do you get to see her much?"

She put the wrapping from the flowers into a small bin and wiped her hands. "It's pointless. I see her maybe once a month." She sighed heavily and looked at him. "Shall we go then?"

"Yep. Have a drink first," he said in an attempt to lighten the mood, "and then wander round the town. Got any preferences?"

She picked up her small clutch bag and hooked into Harry's arm. "Pot luck," she said with an expectant, tingling feeling buzzing through her veins.

It was so different with Simon, she thought as they hurried out and into the charming streets of Chichester.

***

That evening, Jenny kicked off her shoes and poured herself a glass of wine. She asked Alexa to play some mood music and turn her lights on to her chosen romantic scene. Then she sat in her swivel recliner and thought about the whole evening with Harry as she gently swivelled the chair from side to side.

Harry had been an absolute delight to be with. He was funny, unpretentious, absorbing, interesting, no ego. She felt completely at ease with him. Somehow he'd been able to change from the Trojan man to Harry — simply a friend. He'd never tried to dominate the conversation, always allowing her the room to talk, to make jokes and allowing her to feel she was his equal.

She found herself comparing the evening out in the town with Harry to that of the evening at the posh, exclusive restaurant with Simon. In their own way, the two brothers had shown her two very different sides to two seemingly equal men, and she found it difficult to say which evening she enjoyed most.

Or which brother she enjoyed most.

Chapter 11

Jenny was able to set aside her conflicting emotions and concentrate on her work and getting to know more of Trojan's staff as she moved around the site picking up the heart of a company that seemed so at ease with itself. Other workers acknowledged her, often with a cheery smile, sometimes a subjective offer for a night out. She would often tease those men who made the offers, and it was all taken in good spirit and never seriously. There was also a strong rumour that one of the executives was showing an interest in Jenny, and it would not do to mess on your own doorstep.

Jenny had been spending virtually all of her time at Trojan, but occasionally she would pop into Chichester for a verbal report to her boss. The conversation was usually divided into two halves: work and gossip. KJ was very keen on learning as much as she could about Trojan and what made it tick. Jenny assumed it was simply an astute businesswoman plying her craft and achieving real success in almost all of her operations with other businesses, large of small.

"I've had regular updates of course, Jenny, from Trojan. Mister Harold?"

Jenny grinned. "Harry. He prefers that to the formal version."

"Are you close to him?"

Jenny made a face. "We've been out a couple of times." She flicked a thumb over her shoulder. "In Chichester. Did a pub crawl. Chinese afterwards. Nothing in it, KJ — we're just friends."

KJ's expression darkened. "Don't be so naïve, Jenny. Harry, as you call him, has equal standing in Trojan with his brother, although their roles are a little different. But he's your boss, and you'll be playing with fire if it continues. You could lose your job. And that would not help KJ Marketing."

"It won't, KJ; he's a completely different person once he steps through the front doors of Trojan, believe me."

"I wish I could. And what about Mister Simon? He showed a really close interest in you. Has that changed?"

"Well, he's been abroad on business, so I haven't seen him for a couple of weeks. He's due back sometime this week."

This seemed to satisfy KJ. She had managed to drag a little information out of Jenny and impart the implicit, unspoken warning about messing with one of the bosses. She pulled open a drawer and took out a smallish envelope. She flipped it open and showed it to Jenny. It was an invitation to the gala event planned for the following week.

"It has a plus one on it. I was thinking of asking you."

Jenny frowned. "Don't you have a boyfriend or someone you want to take?"

KJ shook her head in a short, abrupt movements. "None of your business, Jenny. Do you want to come or not?"

Jenny tried not to show a grin forming on her lips by putting her hand to her face and smothering it. She was secretly delighted to get the opportunity, but the grin was more about KJ's discomfort in having to admit she didn't have a man in her life, or that she had a woman who she wanted to keep secret. It kind of made KJ more natural and, maybe vulnerable behind that hard exterior.

"I'd love to come," she said. "I'll have to buy a new

frock."

"Dress!"

Jenny laughed. "Dress then."

KJ nodded her satisfaction. Then unexpectedly she said, "You never know, Jenny, we might both meet someone interesting."

***

Two days later, Simon knocked on Jenny's office door and walked in.

"Good morning, Jenny."

She looked up from her computer and smiled at him. It was a genuine, spontaneous reaction to seeing him after such a long time.

"Hallo, Simon, how lovely to see you."

"Got a moment?"

She nodded. "For you, yes."

"Only me?"

"No, that would be unfair to all my admirers."

"And I bet you have plenty of them."

She gave a little shrug. "Some."

He sat down on the edge of the desk. "Would you have dinner with me tonight? Please?"

Jenny stiffened a little. "Oh, just like that?"

"Don't tease me, say yes."

"Oh, well, yes, okay then, yes."

He stood up. "Great. I'll pick you up at, what, eight o'clock?"

All she could do was nod. He blew her a kiss and left her sitting there practically speechless and overwhelmed.

It took Jenny a while to come down off cloud nine and get her mind back on her work, but now with KJ's warning bouncing around in her mind.

72

Simon picked Jenny up at eight o'clock that evening. He kissed her on the cheek once she'd opened the door and let him in. Five minutes later and they were in what Jenny believed must have been a private hire car; it certainly wasn't a taxi. There was a screen separating the driver from the rear passengers, and the whole interior had that warm, comforting fragrance of leather. It smacked of luxury for Jenny after the daily round of trips to work in her little Kia Picanto.

"Where are we going?" she asked.

"Potagers restaurant near Selsey. Have you been there?"

"Yes, a long time ago. Big family bash in the conservatory. Lovely. Thoroughly enjoyed it."

"Well, that's good then; you know what to expect."

Once again the whole evening went beautifully. Simon was perfectly charming, said all the right words, paid Jenny all the right compliments. She found herself getting so much pleasure of just being in his company, looking at him, listening to him and simply enjoying him — until things changed a little.

He put his hand in his pocket and pulled out a small box. "I bought you something when I was in Zurich. I couldn't resist it."

He pushed the box across the table. "Don't worry; it isn't an engagement ring."

She flicked her eyes up at him and then back on to the box. Nervously, she opened the velvet covered lid and immediately her face seemed to drain of all expression. Her mouth opened in a silent gasp. She was looking at a small lapel broach that must have cost him a fortune.

She looked at him again and then back at the broach. She lifted it out and held it a few inches away from her face. The reflected light from the small diamonds danced in front of her. She closed her mouth.

"I can't possibly accept this, Simon. It's…" She couldn't think what to say.

He reached over and put his hand on hers. "Please say you will wear it. I really thought of you when I saw it. Sentimental or what?"

She put the broach back in the box. "I can't wear this at work. I just couldn't. People will talk."

"Jenny, I know you are coming to the gala; KJ told me. I'd bought that before I knew, so it makes wonderful sense, and the perfect excuse to wear it. No-one will know where you got it. You could even say your old granny died and left it to you."

Jenny started laughing and crying. "My old granny could never have afforded one as expensive as this." She dragged a tissue from her clutch bag and blew her nose, wiped the tears away and tidied herself up. "Now look what you've made me do. I have to go to the bathroom and put my face back on."

"Don't be too long," he said. "I'm enjoying this moment and I don't want to lose it."

She picked up the box and slipped it into her clutch bag. "Not too long, I promise."

He watched her go, unable to take his eyes off her and wished things could have been so much more different.

Chapter 12

"I don't believe it," Sue exclaimed when Jenny showed her the lapel broach.

She looked at Jenny. "You know what he's after, don't you?"

Jenny smiled winsomely. "It isn't like that," she said.

"It usually is," Sue murmured, looking into Jenny's face with a questioning expression. "Or has he already had it?"

Jenny laughed. "No he hasn't; it's more than I dare do. He is practically Trojan Engineering itself. If I got into a romantic clinch with him, I'd be out on my ear. And besides, there's a strong rumour that he's promised to Anna Duplessis."

She poured more wine into their glasses. They were in Jenny's flat. Sue had called wanting to catch up. Jenny related the comings and goings of her working week: the evening out with Harry, KJ's unusual invitation to go with her to the gala event, and how Simon had literally swept her off her feet.

"I've got it," Sue said triumphantly, making herself more comfortable on the sofa. "He wants to set you up in a luxury apartment as his mistress." She opened the hand that wasn't holding her glass of wine. "He has the benefit of marrying into money, not that he needs any, and having a young, gorgeous looking girl he can shag any time he wants. All he has to do it turn up at the apartment and there you are."

Jenny screwed her face up. "Now you're being coarse. There is no way I would venture into anything like that. If I have a man, it will be because I love him, not because he thinks I'm an easy lay."

Sue nodded. "I know, Jenny; since you broke up with Morgan, you've learned your lesson."

Jenny looked wistful. "I thought he was serious." She shrugged. "Anyway, it wasn't to be. It's over, done with and I will think very carefully before I venture into anything like that again. And I'm certainly not going to be a permanent mattress for any Tom, Dick, or Harry."

Sue pointed a finger at her. "Oops! You mentioned Simon's brother, Harry."

Jenny waved her away. "You know what I mean."

"So tell me about this gala. Why has your boss asked you?"

Jenny raised her eyebrows. "I've been thinking about that. She's not usually that friendly with me. Always keeps me at arm's length. But I have a feeling that she wants someone with her at the gala who knows people there and is friends with them. That means she wouldn't be sitting there like a lemon."

"I can't believe that, Jenny. From what you tell me about your boss, she's as hard as nails."

"Yes, in business. This will be social. Different ball game."

"So who will you dance with?"

Jenny laughed. "KJ, I suppose."

Sue lifted her glass and offered it up. "Here's to legs and books — may they be opened frequently."

Jenny touched hers against Sue's. "But mine will have to stay shut." She drained her glass. "Right, come on, my treat for a Chinese tonight, but let's stay sensible."

Sue pulled a face. "Spoilsport."

Chapter 13

Jenny heard the sound of a car horn and realised that had to be KJ with the taxi. She gathered up her bag and an evening shawl, courtesy of a charity shop, and hurried down to the waiting car.

"Evening, KJ," she said brightly as she climbed into the car. "All set?"

KJ leaned a little closer. "Please, Jenny, call me Kathleen. At least while we're at the do. KJ sounds too…" she searched for a word. "Rigid," she said eventually. "Like an implacable boss."

Jenny risked a pointed response. "Well…?"

Kathleen laughed. "I know, but just for this evening, okay?"

Jenny nodded, wondering how many layers would Kathleen peel off tonight. She thought it might make a pleasant and surprising change to see her boss in a new light.

The event was being held in a sumptuous hotel, once a country manor, on the edge of the South Downs. It took about thirty minutes to get there, and during that time, Jenny felt she got to know a little bit more about her boss. Another thin layer removed.

The taxi drew up outside the manor. The building was ablaze with lights. Jenny could see security guards with dark suits, earpieces, some wearing sunglasses. It was more like a Presidential occasion rather than a work's do, although she knew she would never be forgiven if anyone heard her referring to the gala evening in such a way.

They clambered out of the taxi, not as elegantly as Jenny would have liked, and were shown into an area where all guests had to check in their mobile phones and have their bags checked for other recording devices.

"We should try this at KJ Marketing," Kathleen said in an aside to Jenny. "Do you think we'd get away with it?"

Once checked in by security, they were allowed to wander into the large ballroom where the seating plan was displayed. It was obvious to Jenny and Kathleen where they ranged in the order of priority because their seats were on a table of eight at the extreme edge of the room, which meant they came lower down the scale of importance.

It didn't matter a fig to Jenny; she was simply overawed by the sheer elegance and grandeur of the occasion, even to the extent of gazing round the room with her mouth wide open.

The evening wore on and any inhibitions Jenny may have had began to diminish. Her boss was getting on fine chatting to the other guests on the table. The food was sumptuous, the wine excellent and free flowing, and the band wasn't too loud — yet.

KJ was in good spirits too; so much so that she was quite happy for Jernny to take a selfie of the two of them. Jenny immediately sent it to her friend, Sue, with an appropriate, cheeky comment. She put the phone back in her clutch bag and laid the bag on the table.

Suddenly her heart gave a jump when she saw Simon heading over. He had a smile on his face and was already holding his hand out.

"Good evening, Jenny, lovely to see you." He glanced at Kathleen. "So glad you could bring her, KJ."

Kathleen smiled but Simon was already concentrating on Jenny. "Can I have this dance, Please?"

Jenny took all of two seconds to say yes. She stood up

and let him lead her out on to the dance floor, and within minutes she was enjoying his touch, his feel and simply being in his arms.

"You're not wearing the broach," he said. "Why not?"

She looked up at him. "I was too scared."

"What, to tell people your old granny left it to you in her will?"

Jenny started laughing. Simon too. He twirled her around and they looked lost in their own personal moment.

When Simon brought Jenny back to the table, he thanked her and said he would like another dance later. He leaned in close. "Maybe when the music is softer and a little dreamier."

Jenny managed to blush and was thankful for the low lighting in the dance room.

After a while, Kathleen turned to Jenny and excused herself: said she was going to freshen up. Jenny sipped at her champagne, enveloped in a world of her own when she sensed a sudden movement.

Anna Duplessis sat down at the table in the chair vacated by Kathleen. Jenny had seen her looking over several times but she'd tried to ignore it. The evening was going splendidly, Simon had been so attentive and the music, the dancing and everything about the gala ball was simply mesmerising.

She looked up at Anna. She could smell the lovely fragrance of her very expensive perfume and couldn't help thinking how lovely she looked. Jenny knew that Simon would have been with Anna because this was a Trojan function.

Anna smiled. There was a simple, affected warmth in the smile that would have fooled a lot of simpering women. But it wasn't fooling Jenny.

"Evening, Jenny. Are you enjoying yourself?"

Jenny returned the affected smile. "Yes, thank you, Anna. And you?"

Anna leaned in a little closer because the music made it difficult to be heard at a normal level. "I need to speak to you, but somewhere quiet." She pointed with the fan she was holding. "The foyer should be quiet enough. Do you mind?"

She stood up without waiting for Jenny to answer. Jenny's curiosity was enough to get her following Anna out to the hotel foyer.

Anna walked over to a curved, upholstered sofa and sat down. Jenny did the same. Anna laid a hand on Jenny's forearm.

"I need to warn you..." She stopped, her eyes hooding over for a moment, "about your association with Simon." Before Jenny could say anything, Anna held her hand up. "I'm sure you are having a wonderful time with him. I suspect you are sleeping together, maybe not as often as you would like, but you probably think your relationship has been cemented into solid ground." She touched Jenny's arm again. "And this is where I have to disabuse of that notion."

Jenny frowned, wondering where this was all going. "I am not sleeping with him," she said testily.

Anna continued, almost without pause.

"You probably don't know, but there is an impediment to any prospect of you two continuing with this relationship. You see, Simon is an extremely wealthy man. The family own the Trojan corporation, and because it is a private Company, there are no shareholders. "

"I thought his father was the owner."

The hand touched her again. "Simon's great grandfather started the Trojan engineering company. His son, Simon's grandfather. inherited the company and built it almost to the position it occupies now. But Simon's mother inherited the company when her father died. And when she sadly passed away with cancer, she bequeathed it equally to Simon's father and the two boys."

Jenny was genuinely shocked. She assumed that Simon was simply part of the family who ran the company, with the father as sole owner. She knew the company wasn't limited; it was private.

Anna studied her for a while. "I can see you're confused, but the details of the family inheritance mean that the company can only be passed on to blood relatives: not an outsider who marries into the family."

She sat back a little too smugly for Jenny's liking.

"Why are you telling me this?"

"Because of Simon's wealth and his position in Trojan, he would never be allowed to marry a glorified menial clerk."

Jenny reacted in the way Anna had intended. She wanted to strike out at the woman's arrogant assumption that she was a menial clerk. It absolutely infuriated her.

"You've got a bloody cheek!" Jenny stormed. "I am not a menial clerk despite what your puffed up ego might think." She went to stand up, but Anna grabbed her arm.

"Don't you walk away from me!"

Jenny dragged her arm away forcibly and stood up. She was quite angry.

"Whatever relationship you have with Simon, it won't last five minutes. Your bloody arrogance will destroy any feelings he has for you. That's if he has any at the moment," she added curtly.

Anna stood up and blocked Jenny from leaving. Her face changed: her expression became more venal. The bitterness was obvious.

"Simon and I have already talked about a union between our two companies. They will be stronger, have more influence and work infinitely better on the world stage. But it will only happen once we are married. We plan to announce our engagement soon. You," she jabbed her finger at Jenny, "will be nothing but a sad memory."

Jenny grabbed her finger. "Bitch!" she said and twisted it sharply. "Next time it will be your fucking neck!"

Anna smiled. "And your hanging." She wiggled her fingers. "You will pay for that, I promise. Enjoy the rest of the evening, Jenny."

And with that bombshell, she walked away.

Jenny felt the heat rising in her face and tears building up behind her eyes. She hurried into the toilet to hide from anyone who might have witnessed the argument between her and Anna. She didn't have her clutch bag with her so was unable to wash her face and touch up the damage done by the confrontation and the tears that were now falling freely.

She picked up a tissue and dabbed at her face, trying to make the best of a bad job when her boss walked in.

"There you are, Jenny. I've just seen Anna Duplessis. She looked as though she's been in a fight. Looked very angry. Was that with you?"

Jenny turned and literally glared at KJ. "That cow! She accused me of sleeping with Simon."

KJ gave her a blank look. "Well, you are, aren't you?"

"No I am bloody not!" she shouted angrily and brushed past KJ, heading for the door. "I'm going home. I'll see you at the office. Sorry, Kathleen, but I'm not staying in the same room as that bitch."

And left KJ gawping in astonishment, but with a worrying thought taking root in her mind.

Chapter 14

Simon breezed into work with little on his mind other than an email from his father telling him there was to be an extraordinary meeting of the board, without minutes, at ten o'clock that morning. It wasn't unusual for him to receive these little interruptions to his working day. Although his father was little more than an honorary director of the company, he still had a great deal of company service and often acted as a representative since his retirement when preliminary meetings with new businesses were in the offing.

Simon walked into the conference room at the appointed time and was surprised to see the entire board gathered there, including Guy Ford who was the CEO. His brother, Harry was there as well, so with himself and his father, there were four in attendance. The Company secretary, Harriet, was also there but only if she was required to locate any detail that was needed, much of which meant searching through her files or recalling something from the depths of her own, personal, and extremely efficient memory bank.

Ford looked up as Simon walked in. "Ah, good morning, Simon."

"Do you want a coffee?" Harriet asked.

Simon shook his head. "Thank you, Harriet. No."

He sat down, a querulous expression building on his face. The conference table was empty save for unopened bottles of spring water and clean glasses. There were usually notepads and pens handy, but not now.

"We'll get on with this then," Ford said, and cleared his throat. "We have received a disturbing email from Miss

Anna Duplessis of Cobalt Racing. It refers to a confrontation with the young lady, Miss Paige from KJ Marketing, at the gala last Saturday evening."

Simon said nothing, just waited for the follow on.

"It seems that Miss Paige became extremely violent towards Miss Duplessis when confronted about her association with yourself, Simon."

Simon gave a slight shrug. "Women fight over men. It's nothing."

Ford went on. "Miss Duplessis has pointed out that the planned contract between Trojan and Cobalt Racing could be jeapordised if Miss Paige, and for that matter, KJ Marketing, continue their association with us." He dropped the printed email on the table and looked at Simon with an enquiring expression on his face.

Simon leaned back in his chair, obviously shocked at the implied threat. "Oh, come on, Guy; this is just bullshit: a catfight between two women? You willing to let that jeapordised the negotiations between us and Cobalt?"

"Not me, Simon," Ford pointed out. "It seems your fling, or whatever it is with Miss Paige, is going to rob us of a very lucrative and potentially world-wide market."

"Well, for what it's worth," Simon began, "Miss Paige and I have not been sleeping together. Let's get that straight for a start. I admit to having strong feelings for her and she has returned those feelings. And we have tried to keep them separate from our work here."

Ford sighed heavily. "I doubt whether Miss Duplessis sees it that way, despite your protestations." He tapped the printed email again. "This is serious and leaves me with no option but to propose to the board that we ask Miss Paige to leave the site. And I also propose that we relinquish any connection with KJ Marketing."

Simon got to his feet. "Ridiculous…" But before he could continue with his reaction, his brother told him to sit down.

"Simon, Miss Paige is a risk and a danger to us. I've dated her on a couple of occasions, but very soon I began to see where it could end up: you and I at loggerheads and causing problems here at Trojan." He puffed out his cheeks. "She's a lovely girl, but we have to put those feelings aside. She has to go."

Simon slumped back in his chair.

"I think a show of hands will suffice here, gentlemen, if you please," Ford said. All hands went up except Simon's.

His father glared at him. "Simon!"

He knew what he had to do and very reluctantly raised his hand.

"Good," said Ford and asked Harrier to draft a formal letter to KJ Marketing reporting the board's unanimous decision. "Meanwhile, send an email to KJ Marketing explaining the decision, and that they will receive a formal letter for their records." He stood up. "Thank you, everyone."

***

Jenny was back in the office at KJ Marketing when the phone vibrated on her desk. She spun it round and looked at the name of the sender. It was Simon. She turned it off. Just then she saw KJ crossing the office floor, heading straight towards her.

"My office, Jenny. Now."

Jenny frowned and got up from her desk as the phone trilled again. She ignored it and followed KJ into her office.

KJ pointed to the visitor's chair but said nothing. Jenny began to feel some trepidation. She had half expected one of KJ's 'talks', but there was something in her body language that didn't bode well.

KJ passed a printed email across the desk to Jenny. "This arrived fifteen minutes ago. It's taken me that long to let it sink in."

Jenny read the email. There was no misunderstanding; it was all laid out quite clearly. She felt her colour coming up as she laid the email back on the desk. She looked at KJ, the shock and bewilderment gathering on her face. She shook her head slowly.

"I don't know what to say, KJ. Me and Anna Duplessis had a row on Saturday night, but it was nothing to do with my work, the contracts, anything like that."

KJ pulled the email back. "Whatever it was, Jenny, it means we have lost what was probably our most important customer and potentially a very productive time for us because you couldn't keep your hands off Anna Duplessis' fiancé. And now she has issued this ultimatum, that's the end of it. No reprise, no requests for an explanation. Trojan has to look after their most valuable assets and unfortunately we are no longer included in that list." She breathed in deeply, looking a little saddened. "And because you are the reason for us being thrown out, I have to let you go."

Jenny felt something clutch at her chest, stopping her from breathing. It only lasted a second or two, but she pushed her hand there as the shock drilled its way in and left her trembling.

"Your reputation," KJ went on, "is tainted simply because of the dislike of another woman. But in your case that woman moves in powerful circles, and she has the ability to harm you whenever she feels inclined, or maybe when she hears you might be involved in other KJ Marketing projects. And that harms me." KJ leaned back in her chair; reluctance spread all over her face. "I'm sorry, Jenny, but I have no choice. I'll send your P45 through and add a reference. I can only wish you good luck and thank you for your work, your company, and your loyalty." She stood up and held out her hand. "Goodbye, Jenny."

Thirty minutes later, after saying a tearful farewell to her colleagues, Jenny found herself standing outside on the pavement, shocked beyond belief, her world torn apart by a vicious, scheming woman, and with little prospects for her future.

***

Anna Duplessis laid back in the bath, foam bubbles all around her, scented candles lit at strategic places and soft, mood music playing through her smart speaker. This was a luxury she often treated herself to after a stressful day, or maybe a stressful week, but this particular occasion was different. She'd received a phone call late afternoon from Simon. It wasn't a pleasant conversation either. He had called to ask why she had precipitated the events that had led to KJ Marketing being relieved of the contract, which had also led to Jenny being sacked from her job. He asked if she was pleased with the outcome, and would she now be gloating and congratulating herself for destroying someone who was virtually defenceless against the kind of power wielded by people acting with arrogance and malice. His tone had been measured, but it had been brutal. He hadn't even given her time to explain; he had cut the call as soon as he had finished speaking.

The immediate effect on Anna was unsurprising, and she rejected everything Simon had said. On the drive home from work she could feel her conscience getting the better of her. Twice she had almost had an accident because she was arguing with herself and not concentrating on her driving. That unnerved her, so much so that the moment she got home she poured herself a glass of wine instead of having a coffee.

She started wandering from room to room muttering, getting more and more uptight and gulping her wine down quickly. It wasn't long before she was starting on her third glass and it hit her. She slumped into an armchair and felt an overwhelming sadness come over her. Her mind couldn't focus on anything other than the fact she had been instrumental in getting Jenny sacked from her job.

She got up and went through to her bedroom. She stood looking at herself in the full length mirror. She looked the way she felt: bloody awful.

"Well," she said to her reflection. "Are you happy now? Are you puffed up because you've managed to destroy a young woman who did nothing but get close to Simon? Did it really hurt because she was doing what you've done yourself? Are you really that spoiled that you had to strike out?"

She looked at her empty glass and swore. Then she went through to the kitchen and filled the glass again. But as she lifted it to her lips, she stopped.

"What are you doing?" she muttered. "Maybe Jenny is doing exactly the same, but for a different reason. Are you happy now?"

She poured the wine down the sink and went to the bathroom. She guessed this would resolve everything: give her peace and calmness and allow her to come to terms with what had happened and the charges laid against her by Simon.

But if Anna thought that relaxing in the bath was the answer, she was sadly mistaken. As she turned over everything in her mind, her tortuous tone against Jenny at the Gala Ball, her threats, and her own bullying stance, she began to dislike what she was thinking. She started to hate herself. And before very long, the tears started rolling down her cheeks and there was nothing she could do to stop them.

Chapter 15

It was gloomy in Jenny's flat. The light was fading, there was no music playing, no TV switched on, nothing. Like Jenny, it was cheerless. She'd been sitting on the sofa staring blankly at four, unwelcoming walls. She still had her coat on. Her phone had trilled several times, but she ignored it. It was somewhere, but she didn't know where. She didn't care, such was her state of mind. Life for her had taken a huge knock. Her self-esteem had been shattered. She felt completely and totally unloved.

Suddenly her eyes snapped open and she yawned. For a moment she didn't know where she was or why she was sitting in darkness. Then it all came flooding back to her: she had been sacked from her job; the job she had grown to love since working at Trojan and seeing Simon so often.

She shivered and stood up, took her coat off and dropped it on to the sofa. Then she walked over to the light switch and turned her kitchen area lights on. She picked up the remote and turned the TV on, then filled the kettle and made herself a cup of coffee. It had crossed her mind to get thoroughly drunk, but she binned that idea before it had given birth; drinking alone was not a sensible idea.

She went looking for her phone, checked the unanswered calls list — all from Simon — and hit the speed dial for Sue. She sat down with her coffee and waited for the call to be answered.

"I've been sacked," she said as soon as she heard Sue's voice. Then she started crying. Sobbing in fact. "I've lost my job, Sue. They fucking sacked me!"

"Stay there; I'm coming over."

The phone went dead. Jenny looked at it through tear

91

filled eyes and dropped it on to the coffee table.

The doorbell went twenty minutes later. Jenny pressed the entry button and opened her door. She heard Sue bounding up the stairs and within seconds she was clutching her dearest friend and crying into her shoulder.

"Do you want a coffee?" she asked eventually.

"Don't you have anything stronger?" Sue asked.

Jenny shook her head. "I'd have drunk it all by now. Coffee is the strongest drink I have."

Sue took off her coat and leaned up against the kitchen worktop as Jenny made coffee. She took the cup from her. "Come on then, what happened?"

Jenny felt a little better now that Sue was with her. She told her everything from the argument with Anna Duplessis and the resultant email at KJ Marketing. It took her some time, such was the despair she felt in recounting the events.

"I couldn't believe it, Sue. That bitch forced Simon to dump me. And you know what's worse? She forced Trojan to drop KJ Marketing." She shook her head solemnly. "Oh, god, I feel awful. Poor KJ. She didn't deserve this; she worked so hard for it."

Sue got up and took her cup to the sink. "What did she say?" She rinsed the cup and turned it upside down on the draining board.

Jenny shrugged. "What could she say? Because of that bitch, KJ has lost a huge opportunity. She could have shouted and screamed at me, but no; she simply laid it out straight and fired me. I can't blame her for that," she added.

Sue came back and sat down. "What will you do now?"

Jenny looked at her friend and shrugged, tight lipped. "I

don't know. I'll have to look for a job." She looked around the room. "Probably have to give this place up; I won't be able to afford the rent unless I get something as good as I had."

"Has Simon been in touch?"

"He's tried several times, but I've ignored his calls. There is nothing to be gained by staying in touch." Then she managed a smile. "Unless he wants to set me up in a swank apartment and keep me as his mistress."

Sue nudged her playfully. "Nice to know you can joke about it. But come on, Jenny; what are you going to do?"

Jenny sighed heavily. "Oh, I suppose I'll be looking at the jobs vacant columns. Have to sign on so I can get my .unemployment benefit. Then I'll just look around town. You never know; maybe something will turn up." She managed another rueful smile. "If I don't get a job before my next rent is due, I'll have to look for somewhere else to live."

"You could come to mine," Sue offered.

Jenny shook her head. "No, that would destroy our friendship. The last thing you want is someone out of work with no money sleeping on your sofa."

"I'm sure we'd manage, Jenny. Somehow."

Once again, Jenny shook her head. "No, and that's final. I treasure your friendship more than anything, Sue, and I wouldn't want to lose it."

Sue understood, and as much as she didn't want to see Jenny in desperate straits, she knew she was right; it would seriously jeopardize what they had together and had since they were just tots. She mentally crossed her fingers.

Jenny turned and put her hand on Sue's arm. "Sue, I think I'll have a shower and get to bed. Maybe I'll get a good night's sleep and things will look better in the morning."

Sue kissed Jenny on the cheek. "I'll call you tomorrow."

Jenny smiled.

Sue blew her a kiss. "I'll see myself out."

Jenny listened to her footsteps disappearing down the stairs. She got up, walked through to the bedroom, and flopped on to the bed.

Tomorrow was going to be the second worst day of her life.

Chapter 16

Simon parked his car in his reserved slot, lifted his briefcase from the passenger seat, and for some reason just sat there looking at the empty space. Jenny was the last person to sit in that seat. He blew air out from closed lips, shook his head, and got out of the car. He thumbed the remote lock and made for the front entrance to Trojan.

Someone was walking across the yard as he approached the automatic doors. They called out to him.

"Morning, Mister Simon."

He went through the opening doors waving a hand back at whoever it was had called out to him, not even turning round, and acknowledging them. As he strolled across the huge entrance lobby, the receptionist wished him a good morning.

"Good trip Mister Simon? Welcome back."

He managed a flick of the hand and walked straight towards the lift. The receptionist leaned towards her internal phone pad and pressed the button for Simon's secretary.

"Mister Simon has arrived, Hannah. He looks a bit grumpy. Something on his mind, do you think?" She killed the call while shaking her head. It was obvious the boss had something on his mind; he was usually a lot happier than that and always stopped at the desk for a quick chat. Maybe, she thought, it was someone on his mind.

Simon stepped out of the lift and went straight through to his office. He dropped his briefcase on the floor beside his desk, took his jacket off and wrapped it round his chair. Then he sat down, swivelled round and just stared out of the window over the South Downs.

He'd been in Zurich for two weeks and it had been purgatory for him. He wanted to cancel the trip, but that would have meant putting personal interests, which were not important, above business interests, and he understood the need to remain focussed on the priorities. He had phoned Jenny's number several times from a public landline in Zurich, knowing that she had blocked his mobile, but she didn't pick up. It was obvious she was aware that he was calling from abroad, which was why she was ignoring him. He so desperately wanted to see her and just talk to her. More than that, he wanted to take her in his arms and tell how he felt about her.

As each day passed while he was in Zurich, so his mood darkened until he at last reached the end of the two weeks and he was free to fly home. Well, he would have been but the CEO of the company Simon had been dealing with invited him to his home for the weekend. Although this had nothing to do with the details in contract negotiations, it was an element of goodwill that often helped swing the final deal. He couldn't refuse and consequently did not arrive home until the Sunday evening.

His office door opened and Hannah walked in clutching a sheaf of papers and a small package.

"Morning Simon. How was the trip?"

He just shook his head, grunted, and pointed at the armful she had. "What's that?"

"The reports you needed, letters that require your signature. And this," she added, laying the small package in front of him.

He picked it up, frowned and looked at the small jiffy bag that had obviously been opened and resealed again.

"What's this?"

"That came for you, addressed as personal. Security had to open it for obvious reasons, Simon." Hannah had worked for Simon quite a few years now and knew his moods: when to jolly him and when to let him get on with it. This was one of those moments. "I'll leave you to it. Do you want a coffee?" She turned to go. "Oh your father wants to see you when you've got a moment."

He nodded

"Coffee?"

He nodded again as he studied the jiffy bag.

Once Hannah had gone, He opened the bag and emptied the small box that he knew was in there out on to his desk. He opened the lid and looked at the lapel brooch nestling in its velvet cushion, He looked in the bag to see if there was a note, a letter of explanation, but there wasn't; the return of the brooch was explanation enough. It was over. He shut the lid and tossed the box into a desk drawer and threw the jiffy bag into his waste paper basket. Then he got up, yanked his jacket off the back of his chair and walked out of the office.

****

Hannah went back to her office wondering why her boss was so withdrawn, but deep down knowing the answer. She did a quick check over her desk before going down to the drinks machine in the lobby. Normally she would have used the small, private kitchen on the upper floor to make Simon's coffee but wanted a quick chat with Sarah on reception.

She got two coffees from the machine and went over to Sarah.

"Morning."

"Hello, Hannah. What's got into Mister Simon this

morning? He looks out of sorts."

Hannah held the coffees up. "I can't say, daren't say, won't say." She gave a knowing wink. "Once he's had this, he may perk up a little."

"Well," Sarah said, leaning forward with a knowing expression on her face. "He won't be drinking that for a while, will he?"

"Why? What do you mean?"

Sarah looked over at the main doors and pointed. "He's just gone out of here like a bear with his arse on fire. Look, he's leaving."

Hannah turned round just in time to see Simon's Jaguar disappearing out through the main gate and on to the road. She let her arms drop on to the reception desk. "What the f..." She shook her head in exasperation. "Men!"

"Not looking good, is it, Hannah?"

Hannah knew the gossip had gone round the factory like a bushfire: she knew Sarah was referring to Jenny's dismissal and the effect it was having on her boss.

"No, not good at all."

***

Simon tried not to break any speed limits, but his mind was turning over at full speed. He burned his way into Chichester and then had to put up with the grid lock and traffic snarl ups before finally swinging into the small parking area outside the block where Jenny lived. He pulled into an empty, reserved slot, turned the motor off and got out of the car. He hoped the owner of the parking slot wouldn't need it for a while.

He went to the front door and pressed the button for Jenny. Then he noticed that her name was no longer in the assigned space; there was another.

98

"Yes, who is it?"

Simon stared blankly at the speaker. Then he shook himself. "Oh, sorry, I'm looking for Miss Jenny Paige."

"I don't know her. She doesn't live here."

"Has she moved out?"

"Well, she doesn't live here, so that's a clue."

Simon took in a deep breath. "Look, I'm sorry to be a nuisance, but did she leave a forwarding address?"

"I wouldn't know. You would have to speak to the landlord."

"Where can I find him?"

"He's a 'she': name on the bottom nameplate."

The click told him the conversation was over. He looked down at the bottom of the names and pressed the button.

"Yes?"

"Oh. Hi. My name is Simon Daines. I'm looking for Miss Jenny Paige. I understand she has moved. Did she leave a forwarding address?"

"No, she paid the rent due and said she would leave her forwarding address with the Post Office."

"But do you have any idea?"

"No." The reply came back quickly. "I've no idea where she has gone. I suggest you write to her; that way she'll receive your letter. Goodbye now."

Click!

He stepped away from the door and looked up at the apartment block. "Fuck!" It was the only word that came into his head as he stared up at the featureless building like a forlorn, jilted lover, which he was. Well, maybe not so much a lover because he never achieved the physical coupling which would have been a declaration of his true feelings and his true intent.

He stomped away to his car and fell into it. He thought about sitting there and waiting for the owner of the parking space to return. Maybe he could get Jenny's address from him. Or her.

The phone trilled in his pocket. He pulled it out and looked at the caller's name, hoping it would be Jenny. It was Harry, his brother.

"What are you up to?"

"Sorry, bro: something I had to deal with."

"You're in Chichester, aren't you?"

For a brief moment, Simon wondered how on earth his brother knew that. Then he remembered they both had trackers on their phones, which was why his brother knew where he was. He admitted, reluctantly, what he was up to.

"And did you see her?"

"She's moved out. No forwarding address other than through the Post Office. That's the only way I can get in touch with her."

"Well, you'd better get your arse back here. Guy is champing at the bit. Needs updating on the Zurich deal and whether you're ready to join the land of the living again."

Simon breathed in deeply, a forlorn sigh, and started the engine. "Stall him for me, bro; I'm coming back now."

He cut the call and pulled away from the apartment block for the last time.

Chapter 17

"How did you find this place?"

The look of horror on Sue's face was obvious as she looked round the drab, single bedsit room that Jenny had moved into.

"My landlady, Mrs. McBride," Jenny answered, flopping on to the double bed so her friend could sit on the only chair in the room. "When I told her I'd lost my job and wouldn't be able to pay more than a month's rent if I didn't have another income, I more or less left it to her to maybe excuse me paying rent..." She chuckled. "More in hope than expectation of course, but when I said I would have to find somewhere else, she told me about this place. It's hers. She was brought up here. Inherited the house when her mother died."

She got up, went over to the small, sash window and looked out over the street. "Not much of a view, I have to admit." She laughed. "Nothing like looking over a line of parked cars in front of a row of terraced houses. Even more so when it's dustbin day. All those bins lined up like soldiers." She swivelled and looked at Sue. "But there is a positive: it's reflected in the price of the rent I pay." She went back to sitting on the bed.

Sue looked out of the window. "I see what you mean." She turned her head. "Did you know she had this place?"

Jenny shook her head. "No. She told me she started renting it out to students at first, but it quickly became a tip, so she gave up on that idea and offered it to what she calls 'independent businesspeople'."

Sue laughed at that. "Like you, you mean?"

Jenny shrugged. "The downside is sharing the

bathroom. Fortunately there is a second toilet."

"What about your mail?"

"Mrs McBride agreed to let my mail continue going there for now. She also promised not to let anyone know where I was living. She comes over here once a week to check up on the house, make sure it's still standing, and brings my mail over to me. Mostly junk mail of course."

Sue dropped down on to the bed beside Jenny. "Does she know what happened?"

"You mean between me and Simon, or me and Anna Duplessis?"

Sue shrugged. "Does it matter which one?"

"I told her the whole story. Sue, I practically broke down in front of her. I had lost a job I really enjoyed: one that offered bags of opportunity. I admitted that I'd fallen in love with the boss and had a fight with one of Trojan's important clients. Even as I was telling her, I felt doomed. I basically died in front of her." She turned her head and looked sharply at Sue. "Even now I can feel myself welling up because I know, deep down, that I've blown it, and I'll never find myself that lucky again."

Sue put an arm around Jenny's shoulders and squeezed her tight. "Poor Jenny. Has Simon been in touch?"

Jenny reacted to that. "No, bloody hell no. Why should he? I was just going to be his bloody plaything, wasn't I? We both know what he was after." She lowered her head and scowled. "I may have shouted at Miss Anna Duplessis because she's a bitch, but at least she was right to warn me." She sniffed and wiped the back of her hand across her nose. "Bastard!".

Sue laughed. "Oh, Jenny, what a girl you are. Still, knowing you, I'm sure you'll find something else round the corner."

Jenny gave her a sideways look. "You mean someone else, don't you?"

Sue was thoughtful for a moment. Then she said: "What about Simon's brother? You went out with him a couple of times, didn't you?"

Jenny wrinkled her nose. "There was nothing in that. He was nice. Good fun. Complete opposite to his brother, but I couldn't see any kind of permanence in him."

"Was you looking for that?"

Jenny shook her head. "You can't look for love, Sue; it comes to you, and with Harry, that was never going to happen."

"And Simon?"

Jenny breathed out explosively. "Hit me like a silver bullet. Bang!"

"And now?"

Jenny moved her head from side to side in a slow, thoughtful way. "Not really. He's getting married. He would have forgotten me by now." She perked up a little. "There will be other men coming into my life, and I'm sure I'll fall in love with all of them."

"And if Simon came back into your life?"

Jenny shook her head a little more forcefully. "No, Sue, definitely not. It's over. Water under the bridge."

She looked around the room, taking in the faded wallpaper, a crookedly hung framed print, and the general air of dullness. "Time for me to put it all behind me and start from the ground up."

Sue gave her a hug. "That's my girl." She got up. "I have to go now," she said, "my lunch break finished ten minutes ago."

103

Jenny walked her down to the front door. "Thanks for coming over."

She watched Sue walk away down the road, sighed forlornly, and went back into the house.

***

Simon arrived back at Trojan and went straight up to his office. As usual, Hannah knew he was on his way up because she'd been buzzed from reception. She went through after making him a cup of coffee in the small kitchen.

"There you go, Simon. Mister Guy wants to see you ASAP."

Simon groaned. "I wonder why." He took the coffee and thanked her. "Have I missed any appointments?"

Hannah snorted. "Does the Sun rise every day?"

He put his hand up in a mock surrender. "OK, who have I missed?"

"Cobalt Racing. That was your ten o'clock. Fortunately, your brother saved the day."

"Good old Harry. What else?"

Hannah looked at her watch. "You have a lunch date with Charlotte Westlake of Stark Aviation. A business lunch. I've booked it at Potters for one thirty."

Simon groaned and muttered an oath under his breath. "Is that it?"

"Unless you've forgotten that the boss wants to see you."

He looked up at her and put on a desperate face. "Can you kill me now please, Hannah?"

"And just to tighten the screw, Simon: Miss Duplessis rang to remind you of your planned dinner date tonight."

He threw himself back in the chair. "Shit — I'd

forgotten that one. And I never brought her anything back from Zurich."

"I cancelled it. Said you were suffering from Long Covid"

"Thank you, Hannah. I'll marry you now."

"My husband wouldn't approve. Sorry."

He looked fondly at her. He didn't know what he would do without her. "Okay, Hannah, I'll go through and see Guy. He won't be as gentle with me as you are."

She pointed a finger at him. "Don't forget Charlotte Westlake at Potters."

He put his hands up. "Don't worry; I won't let you down."

The next few hours went reasonably smoothly for him, despite his mauling by Guy Ford. As much as Ford understood Simon's infatuation with the young KJ Marketing girl, he couldn't understand why someone in Simon's position had allowed his feelings for the young girl to run away with him. He knew Anna Duplessis and regarded her as something of a catch, both in the beauty stakes and in a business sense. The tie-up with Cobalt Racing was a major boost for Trojan's Racing Division, and he hoped Simon wasn't about to balls this up as well. All this was discussed during the hour long session with Guy Ford, which left Simon feeling as if he'd been mauled by a tyrant. He left the meeting and was actually looking forward to lunch with Charlotte Westlake of Stark Aviation.

When he finally got back to his office later in the afternoon, his brother rang.

"Hello bro, got your head on?"

"Yeah, why?"

"Anna called me, said you couldn't make your date with her tonight. Suffering from Long Covid?"

"Yeah bro, I'm dying."

"Bullshit. Anyway, listen: Anna asked if I could step in for you. She wants to talk business and not whisper sweet nothings in each other's ear all night long."

Simon perked up at that. "Could you do that for me, Harry, and not whisper sweet nothings to her?"

"Already done, Simon. You owe me. Okay?"

"Thanks. I'll pay you back. Promise."

He cancelled the call and gave a little fist pump in the air. Now he could give some serious thought to finding Jenny.

Chapter 18

Harry had no illusions about the dinner date with Anna Duplessis. As much as he would like to have been closer to her, tonight was about Trojan and Cobalt Racing and not an amorous encounter. He had feelings for her, not all driven by testosterone levels, and had once tried to court her. His remit tonight was to fill in for Simon and report back in the morning. It was fortunate that he had no plans for the evening, so the dinner invite was his first pleasant change of routine.

The second change was a text he received from Anna asking him to pick her up earlier. He was happy to do that, although he was surprised having expected to meet at the restaurant.

Third change for him was that when he arrived at her house, she came straight out to the car, got in, kissed him on the cheek and told him she had cancelled the planned venue and booked somewhere else. She handed him a slip of paper with the name of the restaurant and it's post code, which he put into the satnav.

The journey took about thirty minutes, Although he recognised some of the village names as they headed north into the South Downs countryside, he soon gave up trying to figure it out. And he gave up trying to figure out why Anna had made the changes. Not that he minded; it was nice to be out with someone as good looking and classy as her.

The sun had long since dropped below the hills and it was quite dark when Harry pulled into the pub car park. He hopped out fairly quickly so he could get round to the passenger side and open the door for Anna. She thanked him as she reached her arm out so he could take her hand. He liked the feel of her soft skin and the smile on her face as she looked up and thanked him.

They walked into the pub together. Harry thought she would let his hand go, but she didn't. He followed her up to the bar where a barmaid was serving a customer. She glanced over and nodded to them, mouthing the words: *be with you in a minute.*

Harry looked around the bar with an idle curiosity. The place was very like so many old English Inns that had survived the centuries. It reflected the history of England, often found in hostelries that underpinned the legacy left behind by ghosts past.

The barmaid finished serving her customer and came over. Anna leaned forward. "Miss Pope, table for two."

The barmaid picked up a couple of menus from a rack on the bar and asked them to follow her. She took them into a large dining area. It had a huge Inglenook fireplace which was unlit. She pointed to a table beside it and smiled.

Harry pulled a chair back for Anna. When she was settled, he sat down opposite her. The barmaid laid the menus on the table and pointed to the wine menu which was already there.

Once she'd gone, Harry looked at Anna, a crease developing across his forehead. "Miss Pope?"

Anna lifted her shoulders in a small shrug. "I like to remain incognito sometimes. Gives the evening a kind of …" She was trying to find the right word.

"Makes it sound like an assignation?" Harry suggested.

"Yes, but of course, it's not."

He picked up the wine menu and studied it briefly, a

teasing thought running through his mind. "Shiraz?" he said after a while.

"That would be lovely."

They called the barmaid over and ordered the wine. When she'd gone, Harry asked Anna what she wanted to discuss with regard to the Trojan/Cobalt business.

"I don't, Harry; that's why I changed the venue. No-one knows us here, which means we can get to know each other a little better. Simon knows far more about the detail than I do. I promise you we wouldn't have got very far talking about racing cars."

Their drinks came so they took the opportunity to order from the menu: Chicken Kiev for Anna and steak pie for Harry.

"Isn't there anything you want to discuss about, well, whatever it was we were supposed to discuss?"

"Do you want to talk about power to weight ratios, high energy breaking and wind tunnel test results?"

He shook his head. "No."

"Good neither do I."

And so the evening settled into the real task of getting to know each other, and for Harry to try and fathom out what game Anna was playing. If she was planning to cheat on Simon, it could prove to be a costly game for her. She had already destroyed the young Jenny from KJ Marketing over her closeness to Simon and had pushed the marketing firm out of the door at Trojan. It had been swift and brutal. He knew there would be questions about their evening together; the board would want to know the details. He knew he would have to invent some plausible account of how the 'talks' came to nothing. He was sure Anna would go along with that.

When they had finished their meal and Anna had consumed most of the wine, Anna paid the bill with her personal credit card and walked back to the car with her arm hooked into his. She had insisted on paying so there was no way their evening could be traced back to that particular pub should anyone be interested in receipts and expense claims.

They were both laughing about that as Harry pulled away from the pub. He could imagine one of the firm's accountants asking why the company should be paying expenses for a private evening out between executives from different companies.

He pulled up outside her home. It was lit up with soft security lighting. He turned the motor off and turned towards her.

"Thank you for a lovely evening, Anna. I hope you enjoyed it."

"I did." She reached over and kissed him gently on the cheek, "Would you like to come in for a nightcap?"

"I would like that very much."

She touched his lips with the tip of her finger. "It's only so we can come up with a cock and bull story about the business we discussed." She giggled. "Sorry. That was an unfortunate choice of words."

He leaned towards her. Slowly. She turned her face towards him, her lips parting in expectation. He kissed her. Gently at first. Then more firmly. Anna responded with a little more passion. Harry felt himself getting harder. The bugger of it was, he had to shift. He pulled away and got out of the car, made himself more comfortable and went round to Anna's side.

She reached out to him, laughing a little. "I think it's the

110

drink," she said, and tried to straighten up.

He held her firmly as he guided her towards the front door of the house. She fumbled as she tried to find the door key in her small handbag. Then she gave up and handed the bag to him.

Five minutes later they were tearing each other's clothes off, not even making it up to the bedroom, but falling in a heap together on the leather sofa.

Chapter 19

Harry rolled into work the following morning feeling, and looking, a little jaded. There was often a board meeting at ten o'clock at Trojan: more of an informal talk rather than one where a particular topic was the theme of the day. Harry had managed to shower and shave before coming to work, but it was a close run thing: he'd woken up with Hannah beside him and knew immediately he was in trouble if he didn't get his arse into gear and be in his office for the usual eight o'clock start.

He'd made it back to his place with just enough time to shower and shave but had to forgo breakfast — something he rarely did and had also managed to put together in his head some crap stuff about the business talk with Anna. He couldn't help smiling as he imagined the reaction he would get if he told the board members the truth. And he guessed Simon wouldn't be too pleased either.

While he'd been getting dressed hurriedly at Anna's, he asked her why it happened.

"Because you push all my buttons, Harry," she told him.

"Doesn't Simon push them too?"

"Not like you."

She caught him just as he was trying to get his leg into his trousers, pushing him back on to the bed.

"Once more," she demanded and I'll let you go."

He couldn't help laughing as she fell on him. When it was over, he wasn't laughing, but the smile didn't leave his face.

Now he was back in formal mode and trying to shove the amazing experience to the back of his mind; although he couldn't help feeling it was written in capital letters all over his face.

There was a knock on his office door and Simon walked in.

"Morning, Harry. How did it go last night."

"Oh, you know: she couldn't keep her hands off me and we spent all night shagging. Usual stuff." He was amazed that he'd actually managed to tell his brother the truth.

Simon grinned and dropped into the visitor's chair. "You wish. Was it alright though? No awkwardness?"

Harry frowned. "Should there have been?"

"No, I just wondered if you might have felt, well, Anna has a forceful personality. Comes over a bit strong sometimes."

"I can imagine it," Harry responded, remembering how forceful Anna had been. "But it isn't the first time I've been in her company, Simon, so I was able to grin and bear it."

"Good boy. Got anything for the meeting?"

Harry shook his head, thinking it might be better to downplay it. "Not a lot, really. Mostly exploring those areas that were new to us." He couldn't believe he was saying this.

"Did she mention Jenny?"

Harry pursed his lips and shook his head. "Nary a word."

Simon's head bobbed up and down slowly. He looked thoughtful. Then he said: "Jenny's missing."

Harry looked alarmed. "Missing? Like, can't be found missing?"

"She's moved out, left no forwarding address. I bought her a gift from Zurich. She sent that back to me. No-one at KJ Marketing knows where she is either. She's gone."

113

"Would they tell you if they knew? You're not exactly welcome there, are you? You cost Jenny her job. They sacked her — blamed her for losing the marketing contract with us." He smirked. "No wonder they wouldn't tell you." He sat up suddenly. "Whoa! Did you really ask them?"

Simon looked a little sheepish. "I phoned. Tried to explain."

"And did you tell them the board's decision was unanimous? That you voted in favour too?"

"Well, it's a fucking mess, Harry. I've got real feelings for that girl; I really have."

"Have you fallen in love with her?"

Simon's expression changed into a kind of submissive admission that he had, but he didn't answer his brother's question.

Harry didn't need an answer, but it did makes things a little more complicated. He'd found an enticing union with Anna, while Simon had fallen for a girl of little consequence to Trojan Engineering and was virtually promised to one who was.

He got up from his chair, went round the desk and put his hand on Simon's shoulder. "You need to get her out of your system, bro; you'll be no good to us until you do. I'll see you at the board meeting."

He left his brother sitting there knowing that between the two of them, they'd both fallen into a trap that was not deliberate, not of their own choosing and likely to be a ticking bomb in Trojan's future.

***

The evenings were drawing in and Jenny could feel the cold creeping into her room as the sun went down. Although there was central heating in the house, the tenants had no control over it, which meant the temperature was never that high. She would put an extra layer on when she was in her room at night. Sometimes she would get into bed and watch a film on her laptop or read a book. Her mind was never far from thoughts of Simon and how life could have been so different if she hadn't lost her job.

In the mornings, Jenny would grab the bathroom as early as she could, quick shower, dress and hurry out of the house to grab a cheap breakfast in town and begin the search for a job. The agencies had plenty of vacancies on their books, but those for which Jenny could have applied required a reference, and although she had received one with her P45, she doubted whether KJ would provide one that was an improvement on what she had already had. She had seen references from applicants at KJ Marketing where what the reference never mentioned was more than sufficient to reject the applicant. So for her it was a non-starter.

That meant trawling round the town looking for shop window ads or sitting in a café with a newspaper and looking at the jobs vacant column. Nothing seemed to be going right, and the dreary weather was not helping either: everything seemed so pointless. Her dwindling resources were becoming a problem too, and she even thought she could end up at one of those charity places that provided meals for the homeless. Not that she could claim to be homeless: just stony broke.

Then she passed by a café that had a card in the window: *Kitchen help needed.* She nearly missed it. But she stopped and thought about it. Then, just as she was about to move on, a young man came out of the café and started removing debris from the tables out front. Jenny had always been amused at how the country was slowly turning to café culture: even sitting out front at the tables in the middle of winter.

"I won't be a moment," he said to her. "Just clearing up after the morning rush." He studied her briefly, then glanced at the card. "You looking for a job?" he asked. "I saw you looking at the card as I came through from out back." He pointed over his shoulder with his thumb.

"Do I look that desperate?" she said bluntly.

He shrugged. "Suit yourself, sweetness." He flapped a hand at her. "But at least you'll be warm and well fed. And you look like you could do with a decent meal," he added as he scooped up a few more plates and made his way back into the café.

She hurried away, annoyed and a little embarrassed at being told she look underfed. He might just as well have called her skinny, which she wasn't.

Then she saw her reflection in a shop window and stopped. How many times had she seen herself like that and taken no notice, she wondered. But this time she stopped and looked, and what she was seeing was a drooping figure, shoulders slumped, head down. No, she didn't look skinny, but what she could see was not impressive. She felt guilty then for being rude to the lad at the café, so she turned on her heel and went back.

It was warm inside the café and there was a lovely smell of coffee in the air. There were not too many customers, so finding a seat was not difficult. The lad saw her and raised his hand. He was behind the counter but came over.

"We are not doing waiter service at the moment. We might do if we can recruit more staff." He said it lightly

116

with a hint of irony. "It's difficult to get them these days; they just seem to walk on by. But for you my homeless one, I'll make an exception. What would you like?"

"A flat white and a job."

He raised his head in surprise. "Oh, right." It was a slow, measured comment. "I'll get your coffee and you can come through to the kitchen for an interview."

"Really? Just like that?"

He nodded and smiled. "Yes, really." He walked away but beckoned her. "You might as well come through now if you really want a job."

She was beginning to like him already even though he was quite effeminate. She wondered if he was Gay; he had that *joie de vivre* that many Gay people are blessed with. She followed him through to the kitchen.

"Julian, we have a lamb to the slaughter here my darling: a poor waif I picked up on the street. Needs a job and a coffee."

The man she called Julian was cooking something over a gas ring. He stopped and looked over briefly, then turned the flame down. He picked up a tea towel and wiped his hands.

"So, you're looking for a job," he said to Jenny.

She felt a bit tongue-tied. "Well, I suppose I am really. I need work anyway."

He poked a finger out. "Has Motty introduced himself yet?"

Motty smiled at Jenny. "Sorry my darling, my name is Maurice, but I prefer Motty." He held out a limp hand. Jenny shook it lightly.

"I'm Jenny."

"Well, Jenny." This was Julian. "When can you start?"

117

Jenny's mouth opened in shock. "Just like that? What about the interview?"

Julian pouted. "Are you serious? Can you wash up and clean tables?"

"Yes."

"Good. When can you start then? Before or after your coffee?"

Jenny didn't know what to think at first; it was surreal. Then she started chuckling and something seemed to change inside her. It was like a load had been lifted from her shoulders, just by being in their company.

Motty put a hand on her shoulder. "Right my darling, find yourself a coat hook and then grab an apron from that cupboard over there, while I get you a lovely cup of coffee."

Chapter 20

"Where?" Sue asked when Jenny told her she had a job.

"A café off East Street. Baffins Lane?"

"That's not far from the Salon. What's it called?"

"Restawhile."

Sue screwed her face up as she tried to visualise exactly where Baffins Lane was. "I'll have to come over there and find you. Do you get a break later?"

Jenny chuckled. "I doubt it. Well, not until I've been here for a while. Look, I'll have to hang up. Why not pop in during your lunch break?"

"Sure thing if I can. Bye."

The phone call ended. Jenny pushed the phone into the pocket beneath her apron and flushed the toilet. She'd tried to be quick; she didn't want Motty or Julian thinking she was skiving off on her first day.

She hurried into the kitchen, put on her Marigold gloves, and started on the pots and pans Julian had left for her as Motty came in.

"Leave those, Jenny. Load the dishwasher with the crockery and dishes sweetheart, then come out front and help me."

"Serving?"

He came up beside her. "Unless you want to do some dancing." He tapped her gently on the bottom. "Out front, my darling, there's a good girl."

He flounced away waving a hand in the air and not a care in the world.

Despite getting a gentle tap on her bottom, Jenny didn't mind. If a straight guy had done that, she would have slapped him. And as she thought of that, she thought about her fight with Anna Duplessis and felt the colour rising in her cheeks.

She loaded the dishwasher and hurried out front to watch a master craftsman working the punters and charming them with his particular brand of repartee.

It was after the lunchtime rush when Jenny was able to grab a bite to eat out in the kitchen while Julian kept an eye open at the tables. Motty came breezing in.

"Lady friend out there for you, Jenny. Is she straight?"

Jenny put her knife and fork down. "As a die," she said with a mouthful of food and trying not to laugh. "Can I...?"

"Of course sweetheart. I'll tell her to come through." He turned and disappeared, bringing Sue in a few seconds later.

Jenny was still finishing her mouthful as she hugged Sue.

"So, what do you think?" she said eventually.

Sue did a quick pirouette. "It's a job, Jenny, and that's the important thing."

Motty tapped Sue on the shoulder. "It's a calling, my darling, a calling."

Jenny put her hand to her mouth and swallowed the remains of her food. "Oh, Sue, this is my boss, Motty."

Sue shook his hand. "Nice to meet you, Motty. My name's Sue."

"I know, sweetheart." He flicked his hand in the air like swatting away a fly. "Now don't keep Jenny too long, there's a dear."

Sue watched him swivel his hips as he waltzed out of the kitchen. She turned and looked at Jenny, a face a picture of amusement.

"Does he…?"

Jenny nodded. "Yes, all the time. The punters love it." She grinned. "So do I."

Once again, Sue looked around. "Well, it certainly looks pristine in here. Is this your doing?"

Jenny chuckled. "Come on, Sue; I've only been here five minutes. It's those two: they work like Trojans." Her hand shot up to her face. "Oops! I shouldn't have said. Well, no matter; you know what I mean."

"Do you think you'll like it here?"

She shook her head. "It's not really a case of liking it, Sue: it's a job. I know it isn't exactly a career move, is it? I'll probably stick it out until something better comes along."

Sue nodded. "I know what you mean. Can't really use your marketing skills in here, can you?"

"Those two market themselves, believe me. I couldn't compete with that."

Sue looked at her watch. "I need to go, but I want to know if you've spoken to Simon yet?"

Jenny frowned. "Why would I do that?"

"Because you fell in love with him. He hurt you pretty bad, I know, but I think you still have feelings for him."

"Well I'm not going down that rabbit hole. It's finished. Over. In a month or two I will have forgotten everything about him." She swept a hand in a loop. "This will be my new love."

Sue grinned. "Two Gay boys and a mountain of dishes. What could go wrong?"

Jenny stood up. "Time to throw you out." She gave Sue a big hug. "Thanks for coming. I wouldn't mind a night out on Saturday if you're not busy writing books."

"Sure. I'll give you a call. And don't forget."

"What?"

"Legs and books, may they be opened frequently."

She hurried out of the kitchen leaving Jenny with a big smile on her face.

***

Simon met Anna on Bognor Sea Front. The sun was shining, there was no wind or rain. The sea was flat calm. People were strolling along the promenade, some cycling, others pushing wheelchairs. There were dog walkers, little tots with their ice creams or sticks of candy floss. The sense of contentment was discernible and almost catching, but not in Simon and Anna's case.

"I've been asked to stand down," Simon was saying as he stared at the scene in front of him. "The board want to bring in someone to replace me."

"That's really sad, Simon. What will you do?"

He puffed out his cheeks. "Probably buy a McLaren and roar around Europe trying to forget everything."

Simon had asked Anna to meet him in a public place because he'd planned to tell her the truth about his feelings for Jenny, and to tell her there would never be an engagement, and there never had been. Anna caught herself thinking about her coupling with Harry and knew she couldn't complain or cause a scene because she now knew where her true feelings lay.

Simon had been surprised at how easy it had been, not realising that Anna's doleful acceptance was due to her affection for his brother and the realisation of the kind of person she had become as a result of Simon's stinging words.

"Buying a McLaren won't solve anything, Simon;

you'll just have to find your girlfriend and win her back."

"She is not my girlfriend, Anna. It's over, finished, done for."

She turned towards him.

"Simon, I've seen the way you looked at her on the few occasions I was there. That evening in the restaurant on the Downs? And the way you danced with her at the Gala Ball. You never looked at me like that. If you don't grab her now, you'll regret it. You might bump into her in a few years' time in town, or down here pushing a stroller. She'll have a couple of kids with her. Not yours of course. She'll listen while you explain how sorry you were not finding her and declaring your true feelings. She'll probably smile and say how happy she is, not believing it for a moment. Then she'll wish you all the best and walk away. Just like you're doing now," she added.

"Wow, I walked into that, didn't I?"

"We both walked into something neither of us were prepared for. Or even trained for, for that matter."

He gave her a strange look.

"What do you mean?"

She told him how his damning words had pierced her on the day he'd phoned and bawled her out.

"You were right in what you said about me. It gave me a real pause for thought. I ended up not liking the kind of person I'd become. It was a pretentious layer on my character: one that was not really me."

She lowered her head and sniffed, then rubbed her nose with the back of her hand.

"And you, Simon, wasn't prepared for a girl like Jenny. Your conquests were all passing trophies for you. Like most men," she said a little unkindly. "Handling true love

123

was a layer in your character that was missing. So you see; we both fucked up."

She stood up. "I'm going now, Simon. It might help if you can persuade the board to resurrect the deal between us and Trojan and get KJ Marketing back on board. If you've left the Company, there shouldn't be any problem you sleeping with Jenny now. If she'll have you back, of course." She reached down and kissed him gently on top of his head.

"Goodbye, Simon. And good luck. I mean it."

Chapter 21

Simon made the break from Trojan official and was now effectively unemployed. Not that it was a problem because of his wealth and the fact that he would always, by right, collect a share of the Company profits as one of the owners. The fact that Trojan had to employ a replacement for him at a significantly higher salary than the shop floor workers did kind of rattle the board members. But it was done and he had agreed to waive his share of the annual dividend until he was invited back. A bit like penal servitude without the pain of actually serving a prison sentence. But for Simon, the pain of losing Jenny was enough; it was mind numbing.

Simon knew he could afford to hire the most expensive private investigator to find Jenny, but he believed that it would be seen as the easiest option for him. He could imagine how Jenny would react if she thought she had been followed covertly by someone Simon had paid. But to search for her himself, on his own, was an option that he believed would be far better, although he hadn't a clue how or where to begin, and the only place he could think of was KJ Marketing, despite his previous attempts.

Kathleen Johnson was surprised when she received a call from him asking if she would agree to meet him either in her office or at a café in the town. She decided a café would be better because she could get up and walk away if he was wasting her time.

She asked him to meet her at the M&S café on the upper floor in East Street. She managed to grab an empty table overlooking the precinct, which was where she was sitting when he walked in.

"Morning, Kathleen. Can I get you a coffee?"

"Tea please, Simon."

He came back five minutes later carrying a tray. He emptied it methodically, placing each piece carefully, playing for time while hoping there would be a good outcome to their chat. In his heart he doubted it. He poured tea for both of them. Kathleen helped herself to milk, lifted the cup and took a sip.

"Well," she said, "why did you want to talk to me?"

He saw frigidity in her manner: a defensive posture; a warning that this would not be easy.

"For what it's worth, Kathleen," he began, "I want to apologise for the way things turned out." He opened his hands and shrugged. "I can only say it was never my intention for this to happen, and I do realise what a blow it must have been to lose the contract. It was a board decision," he added lamely.

"With which you agreed and voted accordingly," she told him tartly.

"I know, but I had no choice."

"We all have a choice, Simon. Yours was to throw KJ Marketing out. And as a result of that, I had to let Jenny go."

"That was your choice. I'm sure you didn't want to do it."

She grimaced and lifted her cup to hide her discomfort at having that fact pointed out to her.

"So why are you here, Simon? Just to apologise?"

He shook his head. "No, I want to find Jenny."

Kathleen frowned. "And what makes you think she wants to be found?"

"When I find her, she'll tell me one way or the other.

126

But I want to find her." He touched his chest with an open hand. "I need to tell her how I feel."

"You want to make amends, is that it?"

"No. I love her, and I want to tell her that."

"And then what? Sweep her off her feet and install her in your mansion while you carry on at Trojan and continue sleeping with Anna Duplessis?"

He could see Kathleen was in no mood to be persuaded, but he had to try.

"I am not sleeping with Anna Duplessis and neither am I engaged to her, and never have been. I don't work at Trojan anymore. I was asked to leave, which means I am unemployed."

"Like Jenny no doubt."

"Is she?"

"I don't know," she admitted.

"If you don't know that, then you can't know where she lives," he said to her.

Kathleen shook her head. She was feeling a little contrite, knowing she was acting belligerently and being non-receptive. But she also had feelings for Jenny and felt desperately sorry for her. She realised that because of his declaration of love for her and his admission that he was never engaged to Anna Duplessis, there was a chance that he could help Jenny if he was allowed back into her life.

"Yes, you're right," she said, her voice softening noticeably. I don't know where she is or what she's up to."

Simon sagged visibly and sank back into his chair. He groaned. "That's a bugger."

"There might be a way," Kathleen told him.

His spirits lifted straight away. "How?"

"She has a friend: a girl called Sue."

"The book girl?"

It was Kathleen's turn to show a change. "Do you know her?"

"No, not personally. But I met her and Jenny some months ago at the Goodwood Revival. They were doing a book stall together." He thought back to those happy moments and the banter. "I was running a Trojan stall with my brother, Harry. We had a laugh: you know, the usual boy/girl thing." He paused. "So, where can I find her?"

Kathleen chuckled and shook her head. "I'm sorry, but I don't know. All I do know is that she works as a hairdresser somewhere here in town."

"So all I've got to do is visit every hairdresser in Chichester and ask if there's a girl named Sue working there."

He laughed at that. Kathleen laughed too.

"Let me ask her friends at the office. I know they won't tell me where she's living — that's if they even know — but they may know where Sue works."

"Fingers crossed."

"Give me a moment," she said, and got up from the table. "I'll be back."

Simon watched her walk away and felt a little happier. He sensed that Kathleen was warming to the idea of helping him find Jenny. And now he was on tenterhooks in case it all came to nothing.

Eventually, Kathleen came back and sat down.

"I called one of my staff at the office. Jenny's friend, Sue, works at Bubbles." She pointed at the window. It's in South Street, so why don't you go along and ask."

He wanted to reach over and kiss her, but at the same time he felt flattened by an inertia that he didn't understand. The prospect of walking into a hairdressing salon and asking for Sue seemed to destroy his usual confidence. He couldn't do it.

Kathleen could see the dilemma; it was written all over his face. She reached her hand over the table and touched him.

"Tell you what, Simon; I'll do it."

His eyebrows lifted in surprise. "You what?"

"I'll make an appointment at Bubbles and ask for Sue. The preliminary stuff will be girl talk, but I'll see if she's prepared to meet you. You can take it from there. You don't deserve this, but neither did Jenny."

He was shaking his head slowly. "I don't know what to say, Kathleen. That's really good of you."

She got up, picked up her bag and stepped out from the table. "I'll call you, but don't panic if you haven't heard after a couple of days."

As she went to move away, he grabbed her hand. "Kathleen, there's a slim chance that Trojan might restore the contract with KJ Marketing. It's a slim chance, but if I can make it happen, would you still be interested?"

"I don't know, Simon. You know what they say — once bitten, twice shy." She moved her hand away. "I'll call you."

And with that she walked away.

Chapter 22

Jenny finished wiping the tables clean and sat down for a well-earned break, although break was hardly the right word: it was almost closing time, and she'd been rushed off her feet all day. So when Motty told her to sit down and he would bring her coffee, she didn't argue. He brought two cups and sat at the table with her.

"What made you take this job, Jenny?" he asked as she was taking the first sip of her coffee.

"Needed a job," she answered. "Simple as that."

He shook his head. "Not this kind of job; you're too clever for that."

"Clever has nothing to do with it. I couldn't find a suitable job, and you were too rude for me to pass up the chance of getting my own back on you."

Motty smiled, remembering their first encounter outside the café when he was clearing tables.

"I'm glad I was rude, my darling," he told her. "Julian and I think the world of you, but we know you are better than this."

Jenny shrugged. "I might find the right job, but with no references, it will be difficult."

He frowned. "What do you mean, no references?"

"I got the sack from my last job because I lost them an important contract."

He edged forward. "Oh goody, tell me more. Was you naughty?"

She looked down at her cup and turned it back and forth, thinking of the beginning and the swift, dramatic end.

"I worked for KJ Marketing here in town. It was a good

job. I had prospects. One day we got a contract opportunity with Trojan Design Concepts. As a coincidence I'd met the owner of the business before the contract was ever discussed. When Trojan gave us the job they asked if I could work there, rather than on line from Chichester. My boss jumped at the chance, and I got installed as KJ Marketing's agent in place so to speak."

She stopped and lifted the cup to her lips.

"Go on, darling; it sounds good."

She took a sip and put the cup down.

"The owner, Simon Daines, was to be my boss." She sighed heavily. "Unfortunately, we got too close."

"And they sacked you because of that?"

She shook her head. "No, it was because of his bloody fiancé. She took a dislike to me and we ended up having a blazing row at Trojan's Gala Ball. She just happened to be an important player in a deal that Trojan and Cobalt Racing were working on. She threatened to pull out unless I was given the heave-ho."

"Oh, she sounds bitchy," Motty said with an expression that spoke a thousand words. "So you got the sack for sleeping with her man. Hell hath no fury, my darling, and your head was on the block."

"Not just my head, Motty; Trojan withdrew from the contract and threw me out. My boss was furious because she'd put a lot of work into securing the job. So, I became *persona non grata* and was handed my P45 and a goodbye."

Motty sank back into his chair, a curious look on his face. Then he leaned forward. "What was the bitch's name?"

"Anna."

131

"Anna?" He sounded shocked.

"Yes. Why?

"Anna Duplessis?"

Jenny's mouth fell open. "You know her?"

"Know her my darling? She's my sister."

***

"Sister?"

Jenny had a tight grin on her face when she nodded her head at Sue. "Crazy coincidence, eh?"

"So, what happened, what did Motty say after that?"

Jenny shrugged. "Wasn't a lot he could say, really," she answered. "It's not as if he can make things right, is it?"

Sue agreed. "Didn't he say anything about his sister?"

"Only that they always fought like cats and dogs, but he'd do anything for her."

Sue pursed her lips. "Hmm; it figures."

The two women were in Jenny's bedsit. They were planning their weekend but drifted off the subject when Jenny revealed the connection between Motty and Anna. Jenny decided it wasn't worth talking about, so she changed the subject.

"Have you made any progress with your book?" she asked.

Sue pulled a face. "I wish. We've been so busy at work; I just haven't felt like doing anything when I get home. It's manic; there's a week's waiting time for appointments. We squeeze our regulars in when we can of course, which means working late. Oh," she said suddenly, "that reminds me."

She took her phone out, turned it on and swiped through until she found what she was looking for.

"This selfie you took at the dance that night." She held

the phone forward for Jenny to see.

"Oh, yes, me and KJ. What about it?"

Sue turned the phone off and put it in her pocket. "I think she's made an appointment with me."

Jenny frowned. "Really? I didn't know she was a customer of yours."

"That's it, she isn't. But when she phoned for an appointment, she asked for me by name. Don't know why, but it got me thinking when I wrote her name down: Kathleen Johnson — KJ. If it's your old boss, why would she want to come to Bubbles for a hairdo, and why ask for me?"

"Well, if it's her, then she's obviously going to try and ferret some information out of you. You can tell her what you want, but not where I live." She shook her head and affected a shudder. "I don't want her to see me like this. I think it would upset her."

"Oh, you're being nice. Are you sure?"

"Look, Sue, KJ is not a vindictive woman. In fact, she's lovely. But business is business and I lost her a big contract, so I had to go."

"If you say so. I'll be on my guard. It's overtime too."

"And you get paid for the extra hours."

Sue nodded. "Tips are good as well, particularly when your customer knows you've fitted her in and had to work late."

"Well, with all that extra money you've been earning, you can afford to go out on the lash with me tomorrow."

"You never know," Sue pointed out, "you might meet someone nice: take your mind off Mister Trojan."

"Here comes a cliché: chance would be a fine thing."

But deep in her heart, Jenny wondered if she would ever

133

get over Simon.

***

It was a week since Simon had spoken to Kathleen, but no news. He was sitting in the shelter of the Chichester Cross. It was raining, which only added to his downcast mood. He'd spent most of that week in the city, visiting practically every shop and department store in the hope he might bump into Jenny. He was at that point where he believed Fate was saying something to him, telling him to give it up, forget her and try to move on with his life.

Then he saw her: Jenny. She was walking towards him, although quite some distance away. She was with a man and clutching hold of his arm. He was carrying an umbrella, and they both crouched a little as they kept close to each other. Simon almost leapt off the stone seat on which he'd been sitting, wanting to run out to her. But as the instinct kicked in, he saw the two of them stop. The guy with Jenny said something to her. She reached up as he kissed her on the cheek. Then he pointed somewhere. Jenny nodded, and he ducked out from beneath the umbrella and hurried away to a nearby shop. Then she called to him. He stopped and turned round. Jenny shouted something and pointed behind her. Then they both waved and Jenny turned round and started running, obviously to get somewhere she needed to be.

Simon jumped up and began running down the precinct. He wanted to shout out but saved his breath. But although he ran as fast as he could, he lost her; she'd gone.

He stood stock still, the rain beating down on him, and cursed his luck. From what he'd seen, it looked as though Jenny had a boyfriend. The way they clung to each other and how he kissed her when he left, was more than a show

134

of affection. Simon's heart sank as he realised that he'd probably reached the end of his personal quest and it was time to end it. He turned on his heel and began to long, wet walk back to his car facing a long, long period of utter misery.

***

Simon opened his eyes and looked at the clock beside his bed. It was six thirty, his usual waking hour and the time when he used to get out of bed quite willingly. But after his experience the day before in the pouring rain in Chichester, he turned over the other way and shut his eyes again.

Sleep wouldn't come despite his efforts to shut out the images of Jenny that came drifting into his mind, so he tossed the covers back and clambered out of bed. Five minutes later he was nursing a cup of tea and catching up with the news on his laptop. He finished his tea and closed the laptop.

It was usual at this point for Simon to go out for a run before getting back for a shower and breakfast, but that had changed since losing Jenny; this was when he would start thinking of how he was going to find her and rebuild the relationship and her trust in him. But Simon was a realist. It was over. Finished.

He went in search of his phone and opened up the contacts page, deleted Jenny and tossed the phone back on the kitchen work surface. Then he rustled up some breakfast, had a shower and started planning not just his day, but his future: a future without Jenny. Christmas was fast approaching, which meant family gatherings: something he couldn't always avoid even if he wanted to.

He thought Christmas in New York would be good. He'd never done it before; previous trips had always been business, but just the thought lifted his spirits, and he wondered if that was the reason he'd been so unhappy: he'd let the disappointment at losing Jenny dominate his thoughts and his life. Now it was time to revitalise the old Simon and resurrect the new. Even that thought made him feel a lot happier. He started humming a tune, opened his laptop and began surfing the Web for Christmas in New York.

***

"You know, Motty," Jenny said as she piled dirty crockery into the dishwasher. "Something strange happened yesterday."

"What was that, my darling?"

"You know when we were walking through the precinct."

"In the pissing rain?"

"Yes. Well, I thought I saw Simon."

Motty stopped what he was doing. "When?"

"Just after you remembered you had to go into the chemist. We were under the umbrella."

"Oh yes, I remember. You suddenly realised you had to dash back here."

She closed the dishwasher door and pressed the 'on' button. "It was raining that hard, I dived into a shop doorway. That's when I saw him."

"Are you sure?"

She picked up a towel and dried her hands. "Pretty sure. It was weird seeing someone running down the precinct in that rain without a brolly. Bloody madness. But I'm sure it was him."

"Didn't get you excited, did it?"

She flicked her hand out. "Might have done if he was a

streaker."

Motty put a hand on his hip. "Then I guess you would have recognised him, eh my darling?"

"Cheeky sod," she said. "I'll leave you with your smutty brain; I've got work to do." She walked out of the kitchen, and amused smile on her face. But Motty's suggestion that she would have recognised a naked Simon did kind of give her the flutters for a while.

Chapter 23

"Simon's thinking of spending Christmas in New York."

Harry had stepped out of the shower and was towelling himself dry.

Anna Duplessis was still in bed, but she was wide awake and admiring his physique: something she didn't think she would ever get tired of doing.

"Why is he doing that?"

He tossed the towel back into the bathroom and grabbed his underpants, slipped them on and went over to the bed. Anna shifted as he made himself comfortable.

"Running away, I think."

"From what? The family? Life?"

He turned and kissed her on the cheek. "Jenny."

She looked surprised. "Did he tell you that?"

He lay back, his hands behind his head. "No, but anyone who knows Simon as well as I do, knows when he's down in the dumps and why."

"He's been looking for her, hasn't he?"

He turned his head. "How do you know that?"

"My brother told me."

He sat up and leaned across her. "You have a brother?"

"Is that so unusual?"

"No, but you never told me."

"It never came up." She started giggling.

"What's so funny?"

"I've just thought of the only thing that ever comes up with you, Harry. Far more interesting than knowing that I have a brother."

He fidgeted. "It's coming up now," he said, as he

struggled to get his pants off.

"You've just had a shower," Anna protested as he rolled on top of her.

"We'll just have to have another one, won't we?"

"We?"

"You and me both, sweetheart."

They lost themselves then, indulging in a passionate session of making love, romping, and laughing until they were spent. And as their energy subsided, and Harry was subdued, they fell into the shower and let it all begin again.

It was almost an hour later when they were sitting at the breakfast bench, dressed and ready to head off to work, when Harry remembered Anna had mentioned her brother. He asked her about him.

"His name is Maurice. We call him Motty."

"Unusual nickname."

"He's Gay. All his friends call him Motty."

"So how did your brother know Simon was looking for Jenny?"

"She works for him."

He frowned. "Where?"

She shook her head. "I can't tell you that. Motty swore me to secrecy."

"Secrecy? What on earth for?"

"Jenny heard on the grapevine that Simon had been asking around. He'd tried the people at KJ Marketing, but those who knew where she was living wouldn't say. Even the boss herself, Kathleen, got involved. Seems she approached Jenny's friend, Sue. Made a hairdressing appointment too, but it didn't work out; Sue was on to her."

"How do you know all this?"

139

"Motty."

"Motty?"

"I told you, he's Gay. He's a notorious gossip and hound dog. He could unearth literally anything. But he would rather die than spill a confidence."

"And you are copying him. Not revealing where she works because of your brother's admirable stance."

"I would be letting Motty down. And Jenny."

Harry could see a softening in Anna expression as she talked of her brother and Jenny. It surprised him.

"Why this sudden urge to protect Jenny?"

"It isn't sudden, Harry, believe me; it's been coming on me for some time now. When Trojan kicked Jenny out, I thought it was a triumph. I gloated for days. Or I tried, should I say. Simon called me after your board meeting. He destroyed me, just like I'd destroyed Jenny. I tried to shrug it off, but I couldn't. Then I started to feel very conscious of the fact that I'd been instrumental in ruining a young woman's career and making her practically homeless. When I realised too that I had no real feelings for Simon, I felt like a real bastard." She looked at him, tears filling her eyes. "I felt evil, believe me. All I wanted to do was find Jenny, apologise a thousand times, and ask her to forgive me."

The tears were falling freely now. Harry could see how badly affected she was. He got down from the breakfast bar and went off to find the box of tissues he knew were in the lounge.

He came back and could see she was still weeping. He handed her the tissues and sat beside her, watching as she dealt with the trauma of revealing what she believed she was guilty of and how much it had affected her.

140

"You know what you have to do now, Anna?"

She lifted her head, wiped her face with a tissue and blew her nose.

"What?"

"You have to go to Jenny, tell her face to face what you've just told me, and ask her to forgive you."

Anna smiled grimly. "Confession being good for the soul, is that it?"

"Call it what you like, Anna, but it's the only way you will be able to rebuild your faith in yourself. Even if Jenny refuses to listen, you at least will have tried."

She put her hand on his arm. "But I'm not brave enough. I don't have the courage."

"No-one can give you that, Anna. You have to search deep inside yourself and find it. On your own."

Anna stood up and took a deep, deep breath. She blew out through puffed cheeks and nodded.

"You're right, Harry. But if I'm going to do this on my own, I don't want to see you until it's done."

"Why? I can help you, surely."

She kissed him. "All the time I know I am depriving myself of your company, it will force me to find that courage and get it done. Then I can come back to you and live my life again. Hopefully as a changed and maybe a happier woman."

Chapter 24

Jenny was sitting on her bed, in her pyjamas, legs folded in that impossible position many people find difficult to achieve, watching a film on her laptop when the downstairs doorbell rang. She lifted her head, paused the film, and listened. Whoever was ringing the doorbell, it wouldn't have been anyone for her; the only person who visited was Sue, and she would have phoned ahead.

Jenny waited, expecting to hear the sound of someone going to the door. Living in a bedsit with other tenants was like that: someone would go to the door, but never Jenny. She started the film again.

The doorbell rang again, this time more than once. Jenny paused the film again, swore and got off the bed. She pulled a dressing gown on and went down to the front door. No-one else had come out of their rooms, so she assumed they were all out. She opened the door and, for a brief moment, couldn't believe who was standing there.

It was Anna Duplessis.

Jenny gasped. "What the …?"

Anna put a hand up. "Please don't shut the door, Jenny. Please. I have to talk to you."

Jenny was too stunned to say anything at first. She couldn't believe that the woman had the bloody cheek to call. Then she gathered her thoughts and fought off the inclination to slam the door in Anna's face.

"Say what you have to say and then leave me alone."

Anna looked imploringly at her. "Look, I know you're mad at me and you hate me; you have every right to be. But please, let me come in and talk to you."

142

Grudgingly, Jenny stepped aside, letting Anna in. Then she closed the door and pointed upstairs. "Up there," she said bluntly.

Anna walked up the stairs to the landing and stopped. Jenny pointed to the door to her bedroom. Anna opened it and walked in. Without realising what she was doing, she looked around the room like someone who might be interested in taking over domicile there.

She saw the bed. It was crumpled. A laptop was open on it. Her eyes swept the room taking in the emptiness, even though there were a couple of items of furniture, but precious little else. The room had no warmth and little sense of purpose other than it provided a home for a dissolute soul.

She closed her eyes and felt humiliated that she had been the reason Jenny had been forced to live in what could only be described as the level between a home and homelessness.

"Not much, is it?"

Anna swivelled at the sound of Jenny's voice. "I don't know what to say."

"Don't say anything, other than what you've come here to say. And you can tell me who told you where I was living. No-one is supposed to know."

Anna sat down on a chair that was beside an old-fashioned sideboard. It was the only chair in the room.

"It was Motty. He told me."

Jenny felt herself sag at what she considered disloyalty from Anna's brother.

"Why the fuck would he do that?" She sounded angry. "He knows I didn't want anyone to know."

Anna put her hand s up. "Please don't be angry with

143

him. I forced him to tell me."

"Why? Why do you even want to see me? Is it to gloat?"

Anna shook her head. "No, Jenny; I've come to apologise and ask you to forgive me."

Jenny was speechless again. She frowned and sat down on the bed. "I don't understand. Why?"

Anna could feel tears welling up in her eyes. "Motty was furious with me when he found what I'd done."

"I told him not to tell anyone where I lived."

"Listen, I need to tell you about me and my brother."

Jenny suddenly realised her mouth was very dry. She needed a drink, and she wasn't going to have one on her own while Anna was sitting there. She didn't really have a choice.

"Do you want something to drink first? I have a bottle of wine I've been saving."

Anna nodded. "That would help," she said.

Jenny went to the sideboard and took out a bottle of wine and two glasses. She filled them and handed one to Anna. Then she sat on the bed again, took a sip of her wine and waited for Anna to begin.

"When my brother was little," Anna began, "it was sometime before we realised he was Gay. My parents weren't too pleased, but I couldn't see anything wrong. He was born that way, and just because other people disapproved, it didn't matter to me; he was happy within himself. Then he started getting bullied at school, and by some of his so called friends at home. I started defending him. I even got into fights over it. That's when I found out I was a lot tougher than most of his peers. I became his defender. I wouldn't let anyone upset him for whatever reason. And that's how I became a bully myself, just like those cowards who picked on people weaker than themselves.

"I was like it at university too, then at Cobalt racing with all those petrol heads. It was a tough world and I fitted in just right. But when I had that fight with Motty…" She stopped, shook her head a little and then carried on. "It was a blazing row actually." She took a mouthful of wine and looked at Jenny. "When he heard what I'd done to you, he came round the house and literally flew at me. I realised then that Motty was a lot stronger than me: my life, my demeanour, everything about me was a charade. He'd been protected by me as a kid, but once he was in the man's world without that protection, he fought his own battles. He literally destroyed me in that fight. That's when I began to think what it must have been like to be in your shoes: destroyed by someone tougher than you."

"Are you trying to tell me you've changed?"

Anna chuckled. "Me and Harry are sleeping together. I don't even love Simon but I was prepared to use him as an excuse to get to you." She shook her head. "I can't believe I'm saying this, Jenny, but I'm an absolute arsehole. I really am."

Jenny was tempted to pacify her, but she held back, allowing Anna to run this thing through, get it out of her system.

Anna was crying now. Little sniffles as the tears rolled down her cheeks. She kept brushing them away.

"I can't say how sorry I am because it wouldn't help you one bit, but believe me, I am so, so sorry. I don't expect you to forgive me, and I can't suddenly make it better, but there it is."

She sniffed loudly, drained her glass, and stood up.

"Thanks for listening to me. I'll see myself out," she said as she put the glass down on the sideboard.

"Where are you going?"

Anna stopped. "Erm, well…" She didn't know how to respond. "I'm going home."

"Why?"

She shrugged. "I thought you'd be glad to see the back of me."

Jenny stood up, put her glass down and put her arms around Anna and pulled her in gently.

"It took a lot of balls to come here and do what you did." She hugged her tightly. "I think you need a friend." She pushed her away and pointed at the bottle. "

And there's still some wine left."

***

The following morning, Jenny went to work with a spring in her step. Anna's revelation the night before had turned their relationship on its head. Jenny now felt pity for her because of the remorse she believed Anna would be feeling. It was as though Anna had metaphorically prostrated herself on the ground and begged forgiveness, something that Jenny found herself happy with. But she was not a vindictive person; she knew that holding a grudge in her heart was the quickest way to self-destruction. Anna's visit had lifted that curse from her, hence the spring in her step. And the evening turned out to be enjoyable. Anna ordered a Chinese takeaway plus a bottle of wine, and they parted close to midnight as firm friends.

Jenny breezed into the café and sung out a cheerful good morning to Julian and Motty.

"Oh, cat's got the cream, eh?" Motty responded from behind the counter. "Had a bit of hanky-panky then, my darling?"

Jenny wrinkled her nose up at him. "No, clever sod. Anna came to see me last night."

Motty's face dropped. He came round from behind the counter and pulled her down to a chair. He sat at the table, elbows supporting his chin.

"Tell me all. Tell me everything."

"Well, she told me you gave her my address, which was very naughty of you."

He put his hand on her arm. "I'm sorry. Go on."

"Motty, that's not even an apology. You should be begging my forgiveness."

"But it worked, my darling," he told her smugly. "Just like I knew it would."

Jenny studied him for a moment. "You're right, of course. We are now firm friends."

Motty showed surprise. "Really? But that's wonderful, my darling." He was about to say something else but turned his head as someone walked in to the café.

"Oh, customer." He got up. "We'll chat later."

Jenny turned her head towards the woman walking towards them. It was KJ.

"Morning, Jenny." She stopped beside the table. "My, you're a difficult person to find."

Motty looked from one to the other. "Another friend looking for you?" he said to Jenny with a wide expression on his face.

"This is Kathleen Johnson, Motty," Jenny answered, still reeling from the shock. "My former boss at KJ Marketing. And yes, I think we are still friends." She

147

looked questioningly at KJ. "I think."

Motty crossed himself. "Thank goodness for that. I thought we might be in for another fight."

KJ pointed at the table. "May I?"

Jenny nodded and looked up at Motty. "Can you give me ten minutes?"

He pursed his lips and gave her that cute look he would often give.

"Of course, my darling, but I'll have to deduct it from your enormous salary."

KJ sat down and asked Motty for a coffee. He wheeled away, affecting an effete glide as he swept elegantly away to fetch KJ's coffee. KJ smiled as she glanced at Jenny.

"He looks a lot of fun."

Jenny chuckled. "He's lovely."

KJ laid her small bag on the table. "So, Jenny. I traipsed round all the Chichester cafés yesterday looking for you."

Jenny frowned. "Why?"

"I met up with Simon last week. He is so desperate to find you. I have to admit I wasn't keen on meeting up with him, but when he revealed all the facts, how he met you at the Revival, dated you, fell in love with you..." She shrugged. "Well, I wouldn't be much of a woman if I didn't feel sorry for him."

"And now you do."

"He said he could have hired a private investigator to find you but felt that would simply be the act of a man who can literally buy anything he wants. He needed to pay some kind of penance for, well, destroying you almost. He called me in desperation: asked if I would meet him. He was at his wits end."

She stopped as Motty came up with her coffee. He said

nothing but gave them both a beatific smile and waltzed away. KJ shook her head, a smile breaking out on her face.

"We hatched a plan," she began. "Quite scurrilous really, but I agreed to make an appointment at your friend's salon and wheedle the truth put of her."

"And did you?"

KJ chuckled. "No, she was on to me in a flash. Lovely girl; did my hair beautifully. Then she showed me the selfie of us two at the dance. I wanted the ground to open up, believe me."

Jenny was trying not to laugh, but it was impossible. She put her hand to her face in an effort to hide it.

KJ started nodding her head slowly. "Yes. Bloody fool me. But she did tell me you was working as a waitress but flatly refused to reveal where you lived."

Jenny breathed in deep and with a big effort, managed to stop laughing.

"I'm sorry, KJ, I shouldn't laugh, but I can imagine just how you felt. Sue knew you were coming anyway, so you didn't stand a chance."

KJ showed her surprise. "How did she know that?"

"Pure guess work. When she saw your booking, realised you wasn't a regular, she got suspicious. She came round to my place and told me about it. I showed her that selfie and sent it to her so she would know if it was you."

"Clever girls."

Suddenly, Jenny felt her pulse quicken as a thought popped into her head.

"Have you told Simon where I work?"

KJ shook her head vigorously. "No, I couldn't. Your friend was adamant that you wanted complete privacy, which was why she wouldn't tell me where you live even.

149

I have to respect that, so if I told Simon I found you working here, that would be disloyal of me."

Jenny felt a warmth flowing through her that KJ could behave like a personal friend. She reached over and touched her.

"Thank you, KJ. Sue was right; I don't want anyone knowing where I've ended up." She told her about Anna Duplessis' visit. "She felt so bad, guilty almost. But look, KJ, I have a job, I'm saving my tips, and hopefully, one day, I'll find a job that suits my talents." She looked over at Motty who was serving another customer. "He wants me to work here for ever. Says him and his partner, Julian, would love that." She chuckled. "But I could never get a mortgage to buy a house on these wages, so I'll start slowly, get a flat and, if the right job comes along, I'll see if I can afford to buy something."

KJ frowned. "God, you're making me feel guilty."

Jenny laughed. "No, KJ; you did what you had to do. Just don't tell Simon you found me. OK?"

KJ sighed heavily. "He's unlikely to do anything for a while; he's off to New York for Christmas on his own: no family, nothing. Jenny, you know Simon could take you away from all this. He's a very wealthy man. You would never need for anything. You would have a lovely home. Contentment. Everything."

"When I worked for you, KJ, I had most of that, and it was all down to me and making the most of what your business had to offer. I felt, well, successful. I knew we were not big guns but making it into Trojan was likely to turn us into that. KJ Marketing was going places and I was helping to drive the train. It was a wonderful feeling, believe me. So now I'm starting again at the bottom, and I don't want any help from a rich lover. Can you understand that?"

KJ nodded. "Of course, Jenny, and I'm proud of you." She drained her cup. "I'd better go," she said. "Maybe I'll come by again, catch you working your way up the ladder."

"I'll pay for your coffee, KJ." She stood up. "And thanks for being a good friend."

KJ came round the table and put her arms round her. They hugged tightly. Jenny felt a few tears building behind her eyes and pulled away quickly.

"Goodbye, KJ. See you soon."

And as she watched KJ walk out of the café, she wondered if she really believed all that build up she'd made of herself. Or was she trying to hide the fact that she still loved Simon?

Chapter 25

"So you're definitely going to New York for Christmas?"

"I've already booked."

"Where are you staying?"

"Plaza. Times Square."

Simon and Harry were having dinner together, sharing their ups and downs, their pros and cons. They were in Simon's apartment in Chichester. He was hiding away in what he often called his bijou pad. It was an alternative to his magnificent country home just north of Goodwood. They often met up at the home of one of them. Their brotherly relationship had always been rock solid, even when growing up as feisty teenagers. Their days together at University had cemented that relationship as each one defended the other, both physically and fraternally. And it was still standing the test of time.

"Dad can't understand it. Says you're running away."

Simon chuckled and sipped at his drink. "Hardly running away. I'd have to find myself a tropical island somewhere for that."

"Still pining for Jenny?"

Simon wrinkled his nose. "I have to get over her, Harry. I let her get right under my skin. I've forced myself to forget her."

Harry laughed. "That's bollocks, Simon, and you know it."

"Do I?" He drained his glass. "Want another?"

"Yeah, okay, but I'll have to stay here tonight."

Simon got up from the armchair and went to the fridge. He came back with two cans of lager, gave one to his brother and flopped back down in the chair.

"I did try, Harry. I even wiped her off my contact list. I spent days, no, weeks more like, looking for her. But she'd vanished. Or didn't want me to find her. I realised that the passage of time was probably erasing her memory of me, and soon I would be just that: a simple memory."

"So it's definitely over?"

Simon took a swig of his drink from the can. "You know, if she walked in here now, I probably wouldn't even say hello."

Harry threw his head back and roared with laughter. "Lying bastard. You'd throw me out the minute you laid eyes on her."

Simon grinned. "Am I that transparent?"

"So what are you going to do? You can't go round like this; you're a wreck."

"You're right. Perhaps I'll meet someone in New York and forget about Jenny." He shifted his position in the chair. "Anyway, that's enough about my love life, or lack of it, but how are you and Anna getting on?"

Harry looked at his brother in total surprise. "How the fuck did you know about that?"

"She told me."

"She told you?"

"We met in Bognor. Revealed some home truths about each other. I promised not to say anything." He grinned. "But I was dying to ask you anyway. So, how are you getting on?"

"Things are going well. I'm hooked, I have to admit."

"Does she feel the same way about you?"

Harry grinned. "She tells me I push all her buttons."

Simon laughed. "And more than that, I should think."

Harry looked thoughtful for a moment. "You know, Simon, I think this is the happiest I've seen you in a while. Not just the beer, is it?"

Simon shook his head. "I don't know; it could be. Truth is I'm having to make sense of the reality of my life. Not wanted at Trojan and not wanted by Jenny. I now need to find a purpose in life, get back on the dating merry go round and see what comes up. But not until I get back from New York. That's if I do come back," he added, and lifted his beer in salutation. "Now there's a thought."

***

Jenny opened her eyes and reached her hand out to turn the alarm off. She didn't leap out of bed but lay there for a while enjoying the warmth and comfort while thinking of the previous evening. She had gone out with Sue, visited a couple of bars and got talking to a couple of guys. Eventually, Jenny found herself getting closer to one of them. His name was Alan. He had rugged looks, dark hair and was about six feet tall. Jenny was attracted to him almost from the moment they started speaking. He seemed attentive, not over the top with boy talk or trying to impress her. As the evening wore on, Jenny could feel her atavistic urges bubbling beneath the surface and wondered if they would be satisfied that night.

She hadn't had sex for several weeks now, which was a long time for her. When she was with Simon she had come close, but so special was their relationship, that she had supressed her feelings because she didn't want their association to be a sexual fling, but more like a slow burning courtship.

She thought about the moment when Alan had called an end to the evening. He told her that he had agreed to pick his sister up from out of town and couldn't let her down. At first Jenny thought it was an excuse to get away, but when he asked if he could see her again, it improved her spirit and she agreed to meet him during her lunch break. He said he would meet her at the café and suggested a walk in Priory Park if the weather was good.

She scrambled out of bed and spent the next thirty minutes or so getting ready for work and thinking about the possibilities with Alan. She even thought of inviting him back to her bedsit. And as the images weaved their way through her mind, she couldn't wait to see how her day, and night, would pan out.

***

Simon thought he would waste the day surfing the net for things to see and do in New York. He started his day with a trip to the gym. Although he was a paid up member, he was also a close friend of the owner, Benson. He knew Benson was thinking of selling up and considered the possibility of buying him out. It was a notion he had toyed with before having to walk away from Trojan, but now the idea was growing in his mind: something for him to consider after his trip to New York — if he came back. After the gym he jogged back to his flat, showered and then got down to some serious web surfing.

It didn't take long for him to get bored. He closed his laptop, got up from his desk and thought about going for a walk. He looked out of the window at the winter sun and the trees, barely moving in the soft breeze, and made up his mind. Ten minutes later and he was walking alongside the city walls, letting his mind wander and not fixate on anything.

He came to Priory Park and thought he would cut

through and find somewhere for lunch in North Street. It was always pleasant walking through the park. Many families would have picnics there and spend time with their children. But the school timetable meant the park was relatively empty.

He saw a young couple walk through the entrance to the park. The woman was holding on to the guy. She was laughing. He had his head bent down as though he was telling her something amusing. Simon envied their closeness and wished he could experience the same thing.

Then he realised it was Jenny.

He stopped in his tracks, unable to move for a moment. He almost turned and walked away in the opposite direction, but as he paused, he saw Jenny look over at him, and by her reaction, he knew she had seen him.

He drew in a deep breath and continued walking towards them. He could see the uncomfortable look on her face and guessed he looked much the same to her.

"Hello, Jenny," he said as they stopped within a few feet of each other.

Jenny couldn't stop the look of discomfort nor stop the blush creeping up her neck. "Oh, Simon. Fancy seeing you here. Out walking?"

He nodded, a little bit tongue-tied, and, like Jenny, feeling uncomfortable. "Yes, getting some fresh air while the weather is fine."

Jenny saw him glance at Alan. "Oh, this is Alan."

Simon said he was pleased to meet him, which was a lie; he wished Jenny had been on her own.

Jenny gripped Alan's arm. "This is Simon. He's my old boss."

Alan looked at Simon. "Really. Where was that?"

"Oh, Trojan Engineering. Near Goodwood."

Jenny hadn't told Alan anything about that, which was a blessing for her.

"What did you do there?" he asked her.

"Oh, typist," she lied. "Got fed up, so I left."

Alan looked away from her and spoke to Simon. "Would have thought typing was a better paid job than waitressing in a café, but I guess she likes it, don't you, Jenny"? He said, turning back to her.

"Where's that then?" Simon asked.

Alan answered for her and pointed with his thumb over his shoulder. "Restawhile. It's in Baffins Lane."

Jenny looked daggers at him and tugged him away unceremoniously. "Good to see you, Simon. Take care. 'Bye."

Simon moved to one side as the two of them swept past him. Already Jenny was nuzzling up against Alan and the pair of them were giggling at each other. He felt deflated. It was as if Jenny didn't even want to speak to him. She seemed ambivalent, regarding him as something, or someone, that was no longer of any consequence to her.

He started walking towards the gate, determined to find out once and for all if Jenny had any real feelings for him. He decided to go round to Baffins Lane, find the café and return tomorrow. That then would be the end of it.

***

Jenny arrived at the café the following morning feeling good. She spent most of the late afternoon and night with Alan. They'd gone back to her bedsit and shared a bottle of wine. Alan thought he was on a good thing. He believed he could tell when a woman was champing at the bit, and he knew Jenny was up for it. Jenny thought so too and was happy to let the night take care of itself.

Motty greeted her with his usual animated welcome. He'd taken on a new waitress: one he'd employed before so she needed no training. Her name was Zoe. He introduced her to Jenny and waltzed off again singing to himself.

Jenny had been in for about an hour when a customer came in and sat at a corner table. She was chatting to Zoe and just caught a glimpse of him. She picked up her pad and went over to the table.

It was Simon.

She stopped in her tracks and almost turned away, wanting to call Zoe over. But she didn't; she hesitated. She could see he was watching her, and she didn't want him to see her like this. She went to the table.

"Hello, Simon. What can I get you?"

He stared at her for a few seconds, then shook his head slowly.

"I can't believe you've been here all this time, right under my nose."

"What do you want?"

"To talk."

"I'm busy."

He looked beyond her to the empty tables. "I can see."

She felt a little foolish. "I can't talk to you."

"Can't or won't?"

Just then, Motty came over. "Everything okay, my darling?"

Jenny looked at Motty. "This is Simon."

Motty's mouth opened wide in surprise. "Well, well, well, so he found you at last." He leaned in and whispered in her ear while patting her bum. "Don't rush, my darling;

158

I'll keep an eye on the tables for you."

He wheeled away with that hip swinging walk of his.

Jenny looked back at Simon but didn't say anything. She was beginning to feel uncomfortable thinking about their encounter in the park and the way she had pretended to not care that they had bumped into each other. She felt embarrassed just thinking about it.

"Was that your boyfriend you were with yesterday?" he asked.

Jenny said nothing, but her mind was working furiously. She wanted so much to tell Simon the truth, but the words wouldn't come.

"Are you sleeping with him?"

Again the silence, but her body language was answering for her.

"Are you happy?"

She wanted to shake her head but forced herself to nod slightly. She even managed to mutter something indecipherable. She felt ashamed, like a child who'd been put on the naughty step. But he wasn't rebuking her; he had no right. It was simply his presence that had dismantled the wall she'd built around herself since she left Trojan. And she was standing in the rubble as her emotions got the better of her.

She whirled around and ran back to the kitchen, her tears falling already.

Simon watched her go. He felt wretched watching her unravel like that. He so much wanted to take her in his arms and tell her everything would be fine: he loved her and wanted her to be with him always.

Impossible now, he thought. She had a boyfriend and it sounded like a solid relationship: one that he could only envy. He got up from the table and walked out of the café, leaving behind the only woman he could love, and heading for an uncertain future.

Chapter 26

Sue had almost reached home and was looking forward to getting some writing done that evening. Her mind was on her day at Bubbles: the gossip, the customer's stories, their gripes and moans, their holiday escapades. It was what made her day such an enjoyable experience. It also provided all manner of ideas for her children's books. All manner of thoughts was on her mind as she approached the door of her house.

It was dark and gloomy, a hint of rain in the wind. She hunched her shoulders forward and pulled her door key from her pocket as the security light came on and flooded the small porch in brightness.

And there was Jenny, sitting slumped in the porch, knees up against her chin and her arms wrapped round her legs. Seeing her there so suddenly startled Sue.

"Oh my goodness, Jenny, you frightened me."

Jenny looked wretched. It was obvious she'd been crying. She struggled to her feet.

"Sorry, Sue, but I needed to see you."

She moved out of the way so Sue could unlock the door and let them both in. Jenny followed her and pushed the door closed. Sue turned the hallway light on and took her coat off. She hung it up and dropped her door keys on a small shelf and then looked at Jenny.

"You look awful. Do you want a drink?"

Jenny knew that Sue was giving her the option of a glass of wine. She smiled thinly and shook her head.

"Nothing yet, Sue; I just want to talk."

They went through to the kitchen where Sue filled a kettle and plugged it in. Then she took two cups and made coffee for both of them, even though Jenny had said she didn't want anything. Neither of them spoke while Sue was doing that.

"Come on," Sue said, handing Jenny her coffee. "Let's go through and you can tell me all about it."

"I saw Simon today," Jenny said as she sat down on the sofa. She put her cup down on the coffee table. "He came into the café."

"Oh my goodness. So what happened?"

Jenny told her. It should have taken just a couple of minutes, but she was so upset in the retelling of the story, including the encounter in the park, that she kept bubbling up.

"I couldn't even admit that me and Alan were an item; my mouth just wouldn't work. It was awful."

"Did you and Alan sleep together last night?"

Jenny looked mortified as she nodded.

"When Simon asked me if I'd slept with Alan, I felt so ashamed. It was as though I had been unfaithful to him and he'd caught me out."

"Well, you weren't unfaithful to him for goodness sake, Jenny. You'd dumped him because he'd let you down and, well, basically, he was two-timing you and Anna." She reached over and grabbed Jenny's hand. "You were not unfaithful, were you?"

Jenny shook her head, but still looked glum.

"And now I don't want anything to do with Alan, but I don't know how to tell him." She started crying softly. "It's a bloody mess."

"You still want Simon."

Jenny looked Sue in the eye and her face softened. "Yes. More than ever now."

"So tell him."

"I can't. And from the way he looked at me before I ran, he won't want anything more to do with me."

The two women were silent for a while, each one with different thoughts running through their minds.

"How did you get into this mess, Jenny?" Sue asked without accusation. "All you did was to follow your instincts; your natural attraction to a man. Not all men, but when you see someone and, well, those urges take over, it's difficult to control them." She took a breath. "We do, anyway, otherwise we'd all be screwing like rabbits."

Jenny laughed. "I can see us know, lined up in shop doorways, supermarket isles, jumping away. All over the park."

Sue was glad she managed to make Jenny finally crack a smile. "You fell for Simon, and you fell for Alan. It happens."

Jenny stopped laughing. "But that's the thing, Sue; I fell for Simon, but only really fancied Alan. I reckon we would have lasted a few months — tops."

Sue could understand the reasoning. It's what led to marriage breakups: one partner fancying someone else and failing to control the urges. The result was always devastating for at least one of the parties. And in this case it looked like Jenny was the loser.

"What will you do now?" Sue asked Jenny eventually.

Jenny blew her cheeks out. "Do?" She shrugged her shoulders. "There's nothing I can do. I've got to tell Alan it's over, and I still have to work."

"When will you tell Alan?"

"I'll ring him later. It's a bit cowardly, I know, but I'm afraid if I face him, he'll persuade me to stay with him."

163

She stood up. "I'd better go now. Thanks for lending me your ear."

"Why don't you stay the night?"

Jenny shook her head. The last thing Sue needed was a forlorn, lovesick women moping around the place. No, she would go back to her bedsit, put on her PJs, and watch a film on Netflix. After she'd spoken to Alan.

***

When Simon got back to his flat, he sat down and wrote a letter. It was the first time for a very long time that he'd actually put pen to paper; like the majority of people he usually communicated by email or text messages. But this letter was probably the hardest he would ever write. It was to Jenny. He wanted to tell her how he had fallen for her the day he had seen her at the Chichester Revival. He said how he had never experienced such a feeling before when meeting a woman for the first time, how he had disciplined himself to behave like a suitor: one carefully nurturing a relationship with someone he wanted to spend the rest of his life with.

He said how he had thought of her every waking moment and was overjoyed when she started working at Trojan. He spilled his love and lament on into the letter. The love that he believed was unquenchable, and the lament that she had given herself to another man.

He now believed that she had no feelings for him, which meant he was out of her life forever. He promised that if they should ever meet, he would be polite, friendly and hope she would reciprocate and agree that they could always be friends.

He promised never to try and contact her unless she specifically requested it. And with that he signed and sealed the letter. He wrote Jenny's name on the envelope but no address. The following morning he took it round to the café.

Motty was wiping down the tables when Simon walked in. He stopped and straightened up, one hand on his hip.

"Well, look at you," he said, "Jenny's not here I'm afraid."

Simon thought Motty meant Jenny had given up her job. "Has she given up work?"

Motty dusted a few last specs from the table. "No, silly. She still works here, but she phoned in sick."

Simon handed him the letter. "Can you give this to her please?"

Motty took the letter. "I'll put it in her locker." He folded the envelope into the pocket of his apron and moved to another table, wiping down again.

"What is it with you?" he asked finally. "Jenny has been really happy since she started here. She's got over you, picked up with a nice boy, and then you walk in the door and she falls apart. What did you say to her?"

Simon could see by the way Motty was working away vigorously at cleaning the table that he was getting annoyed.

"I didn't say anything other than to ask her if she had a boyfriend. She flipped and ran. That's all I know. But it doesn't matter now; I'm out of her life and won't be back. Give her my best when you see her. 'Bye, Motty."

He turned and walked out of the café.

Motty watched him disappear into the street and got on with cleaning the tables. His mind on other things when he felt his phone ringing and vibrating away in his pocket. He pulled it out and checked the caller. It was his sister, Anna.

"Hello, my darling, what can I do for you?"

"I'll tell you what you can do for me: you could get here on time, that's what."

Motty looked at his watch and swore. He and Anna had an appointment with their solicitor to discuss a family matter. He had ten minutes to be there. Anna was already there.

"Oh my God. I'm sorry my darling. I'm on my way."

He turned the phone off and ran through to the kitchen, pulling his apron off as he ran. He tossed it on to a chair and called out to Julian.

"Put that in the wash for me please, Julian. I'm supposed to be at the solicitor's office with Anna. Ask Zoe to cover for me, will you please?"

He hurried away from the café and ran through the precinct, his mind no longer on Simon's letter to Jenny, just his irate sister and his poor timekeeping.

It was well after lunch when Julian called through to Zoe. She came into the kitchen with a tray of dirty cups and plates.

"Zoe, can you bundle up the laundry for me please my love. The van's due here any minute."

Zoe put the dirty dishes in the dishwasher and went looking for the laundry bundle.

"Is this it, Julian?" she called out.

Julian picked up Motty's apron from the chair. "Just this, he said, throwing it at her.

She caught it and stuffed it in the bag with the rest of the stuff, tied the bag with a laundry label and carried it through to the rear door where she placed it outside just as the laundry van arrived at the back entrance.

Zoe signed for the bags that were being delivered. The driver signed for those bags he was taking and hauled them off to his van. Then Zoe went back into the kitchen, closing the door behind her.

"Where do you want these, Julian?"

He looked over his shoulder. "Leave them there, Zoe; I'll deal with them later."

"Where's Motty?"

"He's still with his sister. Says they have a little problem needs dealing with. Probably won't be back this afternoon. I told him we could manage, is that okay?"

Zoe said it was and went back into the café to catch up with her customers.

And Motty didn't put in an appearance until the following morning.

Chapter 27

The town began to look like it was ready for Christmas. Lights and decorations were going up in the precincts and the shop windows. The charity shops were beginning to look cheerful with fairy lights hanging up and imitation snow sprayed on their windows. Father Christmas was putting in an appearance around the town, and to cap it all, it was raining.

None of this was a cause of distraction for Simon as he walked away from the travel agency having just completed the final details for his open-ended break in New York. He had considered including New Year's Eve as well, so that he could be in Times Square when the famous ball dropped on the countdown to midnight. He knew he would probably be on his own, but there was always a chance he would meet someone. He usually did. And if it happened, then that chance opportunity was something he thought might just be the salvation of him.

He hoped.

He arrived back at his flat as his land-line phone started ringing. He picked it up. It was his father.

"Hallo dad. Happy Christmas."

"It isn't Christmas yet, Simon," came the gruff, throaty reply. "And it won't be happy with you swanning it in New York."

"I hope you're not going to try and talk me out of it, dad. I'm going and that's all there is to it."

He could almost see his father shaking his head as he said the call was nothing to do with that. He wanted to come round and speak to him on another matter.

"Well, I'm home here at the flat all day. Come whenever you like."

"I'll be there in an hour," his father said, and hung up.

True to his word, his father arrived one hour later. Simon made tea for them both and they sat at the breakfast bar in the kitchen.

"We have a problem at Trojan, Simon," his father began.

"We?" He said that because his father was not a *de facto* member of the board.

"Well, Guy and the rest of the board. Since you left, and it was for the right reasons of course," he added, "we've fallen back on productivity a little. The general demeanour of the staff has changed too."

Simon wrinkled his forehead in a deep frown. "Not because of me, surely?"

"Well, no; you're right. But things were looking up for us. There was a cheerfulness about the place. Our proposed new marketing strategy and the hook up with Cobalt Racing." He paused as if searching for the right words. "And I have to say that the girl, Jenny, brought such a sparkle into our routine lives in the office."

Simon grinned. "More than that, dad; she brought a sparkle into my life too."

His father grunted. "Yes. I'm sorry about that as well."

Simon encouraged his father to get to the point of his visit.

"Yes, back to Guy. He's not happy with the new man who we took on to cover your absence."

"My absence, dad? It was a permanent disconnect. It was agreed by everyone on the board." He stabbed at his chest with his finger. "Me too, for goodness sake."

"Yes, well that's as maybe, but Guy wants you back. He will be asking your replacement to finish by the end of the year. In fact, he has agreed a three month salary severance fee if he goes now."

"That bad?"

His father nodded. "That bad, yes."

Simon let his father's words sink in. The Company were saying they needed him, not just for his ability, but also to lift people's spirits. He chuckled to himself and wondered how he could overcome his own wretched misery and not let it infect other people. Jenny was still a significant memory in his drab existence.

"I need to tell you something first, dad; just to put you in the picture of how I am at the moment."

He then explained what had happened over the last few days, and how his life had degenerated into a kind of subliminal homelessness after failing to win Jenny back.

"If I'm going to help revitalise the Company, I need to revitalise myself, and I can't do that until I've been to New York. Tell Guy I will let him have my decision and my terms when I'm back."

His father frowned. "Terms?"

"Of course. If I'm that important to Trojan, I will make the terms. Guy would expect that, surely?"

His father nodded. "Well, I suppose you have that right." He drained his cup and put it down, but still kept hold of it. He kept his eyes focussed on the cup.

"And I have to tell you we are talking to Cobalt again."

"With Anna?"

"Yes, Simon," he said, looking directly at him. "She's a businesswoman. And as you probably know, she and Harry are an item to put it into today's parlance. She'll be no threat to you." He got up from the bar stool. "I'll be off then. I hope your New York trip pays off. Good luck, Simon."

Simon walked him to the front door. "Tell Guy I'll call him when I'm back from New York."

They shook hands. Simon closed the door and leaned back against it, blowing through his puffed cheeks. What a turn up for the book, he thought; they want me back.

If only Jenny did, he muttered to himself; that would make it a perfect Christmas.

***

Business improved as Christmas got inexorably closer, so much so that Motty and Julian took on another waitress. Her name was Louise. Although Motty was happy for the extra help, his gut instinct was telling him that Jenny would not last much longer in the job because of personal issues. He hoped not, but only time would tell.

Anna called in, promising only to be there a short while. Motty came through from the kitchen. He called Zoe over.

"Be a sweet, my darling. The laundry has just been dropped off at the back door. Can you bring it in for me please?"

He brought over two coffees and sat down with Anna as Zoe brought over something and dropped it on the table in front of Motty.

"This was in a small plastic bag with the laundry."

Motty picked it up, looked at it briefly, then smacked himself on the forehead. "Fuck me, it's Jenny's letter."

Anna looked at him. "What letter?"

He explained briefly. "When Simon handed me the letter, I stuffed it in my apron pocket. Never thought no more of it. And when you phoned through with a rollocking because I'd forgotten all about the solicitor's appointment, I just slung my apron in the kitchen and legged it."

"So how come you've got the letter back without it being washed?"

"That's the laundry. When they empty the bags, they have to sort the washing out. If they come across anything in the pockets or whatever, they bag it and return it when they deliver again."

He held the envelope up and straightened it. "Looks okay. Good thing it never went in the wash; that would have destroyed it." He frowned. "Shit, Jenny should have had this last week." He sat there shaking his head.

"Well, you can give it to her when she comes in."

He shook his head. "She won't be in until Christmas Eve. She promised to work over the holiday, so she's taken some time off for Christmas shopping."

Anna looked thoughtful. "Simon will be in New York by then." She remained quiet for a moment, then suddenly brightened. "Look, give it to me and I'll take it round to her. I'll do that today. This afternoon in fact."

Motty reached over the table and kissed Anna on the forehead. "Thank you my darling; you're a lifesaver." He handed the letter to her. Anna put in into her handbag.

"What would you do without me, Motty? Julian would have been useless."

Motty was happy that it would be Anna facing Jenny. He spent a few more minutes with his sister before he felt he had to get back to work. Anna left with a plan running through her mind and wondered if it would work.

Only time would tell.

***

Jenny was wrapping up a few presents when the doorbell jangled down at the front door. She knew that would be Anna. She'd received a surprise phone call from her earlier asking if she could come round. She said she had something for her. Jenny assumed it would be a Christmas present: a kind of peace offering, she thought, and found herself looking forward to the unexpected visit.

She hurried downstairs and let Anna in. She could see that Anna wasn't clutching a Christmas wrapped gift, so that notion went out of the window. But she was pleased to see her anyway.

The two of them went straight up to Jenny's room. Jenny asked Anna if she wanted something to drink, meaning a coffee, or maybe a soft drink. Not that she had much to offer anyway.

"Cup of tea would be nice, please."

Jenny made tea for both of them. When they were settled, Anna on the single chair and Jenny sitting on the edge of the bed, Jenny asked what it was that was important enough to bring her round to this part of town in the cold weather.

Anna still had her coat on because it was quite chilly in Jenny's room. She produced the letter and told her how Motty had messed up. He was full of apologies, Anna explained, and would Jenny forgive him.

Jenny laughed. "I love Motty. He gets away with all sorts of things. Goodness knows why his customers put up with it, but they do. Yes, I'll forgive him."

She opened the envelope carefully and pulled the single sheet out. The writing was neat, even, and beautifully laid out. As she read through Simon's words, her mind went back to that morning, more than a week ago now, and she could feel herself welling up. She started wiping her hand across her face as she read through it. When she got to the end, she dropped her head and wept. She handed the letter to Anna.

Anna took hold of it as though it was delicate, fine parchment, so unexpected was it that Jenny would let her read it. But she could see why Jenny had broken down as she read through Simon's beautiful prose and his declaration of his love for her. Even Anna felt tears pricking the backs of her eyes as she read through to the end. She folded the letter and waited for Jenny to stop crying before handing it back.

"What now, Jenny? Any idea?"

Jenny looked at Anna. She wiped her hand across her face and reached for a tissue box on the bedside locker. She took a couple out, handed one to Anna with a knowing smile on her face, and cleaned herself up as best she could.

"I don't know, Anna," she said, shaking her head. "I thought he wanted nothing more to do with me because I'd let him down." She put her hand up to stop Anna's protest. "I know what you are going to say. My friend Sue has said it already. But he says he won't get in touch with me, which means he doesn't want to."

Anna reached over and took the letter from Jenny. She put her finger on the page. "Unless you specifically request it," she quoted. "Don't you see, Jenny? He wants you. He's giving himself a glimmer of hope that you will speak to him. He wants you back, Jenny, make no mistake."

Jenny slumped forward; her arms folded on her lap. "Well, he's gone to New York now. Probably find a woman over there who he'll fall in love with. He may not even come back."

"He has to come back, Jenny. Trojan have asked him to go back to work."

Jenny lifted her head. "Really?"

"It isn't definite, but Harry told me they want him back. I think the temptation will be too great. And if he has something or someone worth coming back for, he'll jump at the chance."

"Meaning that something or someone is me, right?"

"You said it."

"But I'm not likely to see him, so it's academic."

"Well, I have an idea I want to put to you, so just hear me out."

Then Anna went on to explain what her idea was. Jenny listened, not believing what she was hearing. And when Anna finished, Jenny shook her head in disbelief.

"Absolutely not, Anna. I couldn't possibly do that."

"Do you love him?"

"Yes."

"Do you want him back?"

"Yes."

"Well don't be a bloody fool. Grab it and be happy."

Jenny sat there stunned. There was nothing she could say, no argument she could come up with, and no reason on God's earth why she should say no. So she said yes and wondered what she'd let herself in for.

Chapter 28

"You did what? Are you bloody mad?"

Motty tried not to shout at his sister. It was late. She'd called in at his house on her way home rather than go to the café where she knew she would only annoy him. But it was done, and there was no way she would let it be undone.

"You're just interfering in a person's life where you have no right. You've destroyed Jenny once already," he pointed out testily. "Please don't let it happen again."

Anna knew she would get an ear bashing from him but was prepared to put up with it. She needed to because she was about tell him about the rest of her plan.

"There's more though," she told him. "But I think a drink will help."

As much as Motty was irritated by what he saw as his sister's interference, he would never be inhospitable to her because he adored her too much. Not that he would ever tell her. So he pulled a half opened bottle of white wine from the fridge, poured two glasses and handed one to Anna.

She sipped her wine slowly as she told him how she expected this whole thing to play out. When she'd finished, she waited for him to say something, but rather surprisingly, he came up to her and gave her a hug.

"You're mad, Anna, but you do have a generous heart. And do you think Simon will come back?"

She smiled. "Yes," she said. "I do."

***

Simon was settling down to an evening watching TV when his doorbell rang. He went to the video link panel on his kitchen wall and pressed the video button. It was Guy Ford, the CEO at Trojan. Simon raised his eyebrows in surprise and pressed the door button. He then went through to his apartment door and opened it as Guy Ford appeared.

"Evening, Guy."

He stepped back and let Ford in. "Go through, he said, and closed the door.

Ford knew his way to the lounge and went through there. Simon walked in after him, pointed to a chair and asked if he could get him a drink.

"Just a coffee please, Simon. Milk and sugar."

Simon rustled up the drink and took it through. He made one for himself, just to be sociable.

"So, Guy, what brings you here? As if I didn't know."

"Yeah, I know your father teed you up. I asked him to do that for me. I wanted to know how you felt about it."

Simon grinned. "Well, my dad made an impressive pitch, like he always used to. I told him I would make up my mind once I was back from New York."

"Would it help you to come to a decision if I suggested we revisit the KJ Marketing contract?"

Simon looked thoughtful. "I have to admit I heard a rumour about revisiting the link up, But I didn't think it would come off. Kathleen's a pretty astute operator; I'm not so sure she would trust Trojan again."

Ford agreed. "I know you said that your dad could pitch well, but I think you might be able to do a better job."

"Really?"

"In this particular case I do."

"What makes you think that?"

"I heard about you and KJ."

"Did Harry tell you?"

Ford nodded. "You are closer to Kathleen because of that. I think she might listen to you. And you wouldn't have to present it as a sales pitch."

"And what about Jenny? Would KJ want her back in? I presume you have considered that."

"KJ Marketing and Jenny come as a package. It would be a positive if you could get them back."

Simon had to back-track. "Wait a minute, Guy. You're talking as though it was a done deal. I haven't even said whether I want to come back or not."

"Yes, sorry, I was probably getting ahead of myself. But will you promise to give it some serious thought? I understand that you won't make a decision until you're back from New York, but we are talking to Cobalt again, and we need your input." He opened his hands up. "I can't put it any plainer than that."

"Okay, Guy. I'll give it some thought over Christmas. I promise."

And with that, Ford's unexpected visit came to an end. He was a lot happier because he believed he had persuaded Simon to rejoin the Company. But Simon's mind was all over the place with the possible and the probable. He was flying to New York in the morning, and he wasn't sure which horse to put his money on: the possible or the probable.

***

Anna was thankful that she could often work from home, although she preferred to be on site at Cobalt whenever she could, and because of the events of the last couple of days, and what she was planning, she needed some time at work before the Company closed its doors for the Christmas holiday. But there was one thing she needed to do to complete and bring the plan together. As soon as she got to her office, she opened her desk drawer and took out an old Filofax she'd for a number of years. She recalled the day she first got it when they were all the rage. She felt quite modern at that time. She flipped it open and scrolled through the pages until she came to the name she'd been searching for. Once she had it, she looked at her watch and dialled the number.

The ringing tone seemed to go on for ages, and Anna was getting a little anxious in case her contact had moved on. Then someone picked up.

"Claude Duval's office. How can I help you?"

Anna sighed with relief. "Oh, hello. Is Claude there? This is Anna Duplessis." She waited. There was total silence. Then suddenly a voice came on the line."

"Anna, my darling, is that really you?"

"Hello Claude. Thought I would ring you and wish you a happy Christmas."

"Same to you, Anna. Now, what's the real reason you're ringing?"

Anna chuckled throatily. "I never could catch you out, could I? But I do hope you have a good Christmas. Honestly."

"Thank you, Anna. Now, when are you going to come and see me?"

"In the New Year, I promise."

"Liar."

She laughed. "Okay, Claude. Tell me, are you still delivering parcels?"

"More than that, Anna; we're a lot bigger and busier since I saw you last. Why do you ask?"

"I want you to deliver something for me, but I can't

send it to you."

"You want me to go out and buy it? Sorry, Anna, even for you I cannot; we are far too busy."

"No, Claude, If you let me explain; it will become quite clear to you."

"So explain."

And she did. Carefully, cautiously and with her fingers crossed that her old friend would deliver. When she finished, she waited patiently for his answer.

"You devious little madam. No wonder you're a success at Cobalt."

"You'll do it?"

"Of course I will. Let me have the details and I'll call you when I've checked them. Now, how about you and I getting together sometime. Helen would love to see you. And the kids."

Anna was quite happy to indulge in small talk and reminiscing, so she let Claude do most of the talking while she responded at the right moments. When the call was over, she felt a kind of nervous excitement and was finally feeling good about herself. She just hoped they could pull it off.

Chapter 29

Simon travelled to Heathrow by taxi with a lot on his mind. As much as he was looking forward to a complete change, there was a kind of flat spot in there that stopped the excitement level building. The one thought dominating his mind was the loss of Jenny, but there was also the offer from Guy Ford to return to Trojan and resurrect the marking project with Cobalt. This brought in two elements that could dull the keen edge that would be needed in bringing in a successful arrangement — Anna and KJ. Although he seemed to have successfully navigated the choppy waters of his relationship with Anna and became friendly with Kathleen at KJs; this was business — it had to work.

As usual, it was extremely busy at the airport, but Simon was travelling Business Class which eased the burden. Once he was settled in the peace and quiet of the Club Lounge, he started to relax, which helped take some of the weight off his mind.

From time to time he would look up from the magazine he was reading and look around the lounge. Anyone watching him would see a man who was expecting to see someone. Or hoping to. Eventually the passengers were called forward for boarding where he was offered the inevitable glass of champagne, which he declined, and shown to his comfortable seat.

He slept during the flight, which helped his body clock. His dreams were mixed, and from time to time he would wake up and then drift off again. Jenny dominated his dreams, but Anna and KJ came flooding in too until he was brought to his senses by the announcement from the cockpit that they were about to land at New York.

Simon had booked an open-ended stay at the Manhattan Plaza in Times Square: a hotel he'd used before. It suited him. It was close to the theatre district on Broadway where he believed he would probably spend most of his time. He checked in and went up to his suite, waited until his bags were delivered before jumping in the shower, and then ordered a snack through room service.

Later that day as evening was pushing away the daylight, he took a walk, absorbing the atmosphere, the noise, the effervescent life style of Times Square, and admired the Christmas decorations, the music coming out of nowhere. It was as if everyone was determined to welcome Christmas, despite the disasters and calamities that hounded life in every corner of the globe.

The following morning, Christmas Eve, and Simon was considering how best to spend the day. There were all manner of day trips available, but none that caught his eye. He did think of a visit to Ground Zero, but the overwhelming sadness that would no doubt fill his mind when seeing all the names of those who lost their lives was not likely to lift his mood for Christmas.

He decided to wander round the shops, look out for anything that might help him choose where and what to do, and take the day as it came. He knew there would be a great deal going on and decided that he would spend some time on Christmas Day in Central Park.

He managed to find a restaurant where he was able to book dinner for one that evening. He had thought about eating in the hotel, but that seemed so sad, eating alone in the hotel room. And by being out he could at least absorb the atmosphere, and maybe get a little drunk, which would help him sleep and not spend hours fighting off images of Jenny drifting into his mind.

He was back in his room just before the daylight gave way to the evening darkness when the phone rang. He frowned, wondering who would be calling. He picked up the phone.

"Simon Gaines."

"Good evening, Mister Gaines, this is Reception. We have a courier here with a letter for you. It does require your signature, but if you cannot take it now, the courier will make an appointment that suits you. After Christmas maybe?"

Simon couldn't think who would be sending him a letter so soon after he'd arrived in New York. Unless it was something urgent from Trojan. That thought concerned him, thinking it could be bad news from home,

"Thank you. I'll take it now."

"Would you prefer to come down to Reception, sir? Or are you happy for the courier to come up to your room?"

"No, my room will be fine."

"Thank you, sir. I'll send the courier up."

He put the phone down and wandered over to the window, wondering what it could be. He hoped it wouldn't be bad news. He stood there for about two minutes when a knock came at the door. He spun round, went over to the door, and pulled it open.

The courier, a woman, was standing there with the letter in her hand. She was wearing a uniform with a logo on the jacket, and the same logo on the baseball cap. She handed him the letter and asked him to sign for it on her mobile phone.

He scribbled a signature, took the letter from her,

thanked her, and closed the door. He opened the envelope and pulled out a rather tatty looking, torn envelope: one that had obviously been opened by someone else. Then he saw the single name written on it in a familiar hand — Jenny!

For a very brief moment he stood motionless, his mouth open and his heart beginning to quicken.

"Fuck!"

He spun round and ran to the door, pulled it open. She was still standing there, her baseball cap in her hand and a beaming smile on her face.

"Hallo, Simon. Happy Christmas."

***

It took Simon a few seconds to realise it was Jenny who standing there, and there was that inevitable question forming in his brain as to what on earth she was doing there. Then he blitzed that and simply stepped forward, pulled her into the room and threw his arms around her.

As he held her, his emotions got the better of him, and he could feel himself welling up. He pushed her away, looked at her again and pulled her back into another embrace. He could feel Jenny's body shaking gently as she cried, but he didn't want to let her go.

But eventually it was Jenny who broke away from him. She wiped her tear stained face with the backs of her hands. Then she gave up and opened her arms to him, a smile growing as she went to him again. Then she whispered in his ear.

"Do you think you should close the door?"

He pushed her away, laughing, and closed the door. "Oh my God, Jenny, I can't believe this. You're an apparition and I'm dreaming." He stared at her. "No, you're real." He

184

stepped forward and took her hand. "You're going to tell me, I know, but…" He couldn't find the words. "How…?"

"Shall we sit down, Simon?"

He nodded. "Yes, of course." He led her across the room to two comfortable chairs. "Do you want a drink? I'll call room service."

Jenny sat down. "I would say a coffee, but I think something else might be better."

He grinned and ordered a bottle of Champagne from Room Service.

"My God, Jenny," he said as he sat down, "my heart is going mad."

"You're not going to faint on me, are you?"

He reached over and took her hand. "It wouldn't surprise me," he joked. "Now, come on; tell me from start to finish why and how."

"It was Anna's idea," she began and told him how Anna had persuaded her to go along with the crazy plan.

"What about your job? Your boss, Motty, was he in on this?"

"Not really. I'd promised to work over Christmas, so when Anna suggested I come over here, I had to say no. Anyway, she insisted on standing in for me: she's working at the café." She started laughing. "I can't imagine Anna Duplessis running around at everyone's beck and call, but she's doing it. And I love her for it."

Room Service turned up with the Champagne. Simon poured two glasses. They toasted each other and kissed.

"But how did you arrange all this?" he asked as they broke away from the embrace.

"When Anna explained her plan, I told her I couldn't afford it and besides, I had no way of knowing where you

185

were, what you would be doing." She shrugged. "As far as I could see, it was impossible."

"And?"

"She said she would pay for it. Not a loan, but a gift. She said she would find out from Harry where you were staying. And she has a friend here in New York State who runs a courier service. An old family connection apparently." She brushed her hand down her front. "Hence the uniform. All I had to do was bring the letter, not that it was necessary." She grinned a little self-consciously. "I was the real package, Adam, not the letter."

"What a package though," he said. "And what now? How long can you stay?"

"That's up to you, Simon; my luggage is downstairs."

Chapter 30

Jenny relaxed in the soft leather seat in Business Class on the flight back to England, reflecting on what an amazing Christmas it had been, She wasn't even sure how many days she'd spent with Simon. He'd persuaded her to stay until the New Year so they could watch the famous 'Ball Drop' above the Times building in Times Square. She turned her head sideways and looked at him.

He smiled at her and winked. "What are you thinking?" he asked.

"The mile high club," she said with her eyes fluttering.

He laughed softly. "Not even I am that brave."

She took his hand. "What now, Simon? It's been fun. No; it's been brilliant, but what does this Cinderella do now that the ball is over?"

"Back to washing dirty dishes at the café, I suppose." He pursed his lips and blew her a kiss.

Jenny laid back on to her seat and thought about their respective roles in life. Simon would be going back to the high octane world of motor racing and a position of Corporate authority, while she would be working at the café — the extreme opposite to him. She imagined meeting some of Simon's executive peers at functions and being asked what kind of work she did, expecting some response that was compatible with the position Simon held. Would those people see him with a jaundiced eye, she wondered. And could she let that happen to him?

She realised that certain elements of their lives would change once Simon was back with Trojan. And would it be fair to him to be expected to devote much of his time to her? Once they were back in England, the reality of their respective positions in life would test them both. She presumed Simon would want her to move in with him. He might feel quite happy having someone he could come home to after a hard day, or after one of his inevitable trips abroad. She would be his chattel, just as she had joked about with Sue. But this time it would be true, and she wasn't sure she wanted to live like that, even with the man she loved.

It was then that she realised that her expectancy in life had been moulded by what most of her peers would expect. They may have all dreamed of marrying millionaires and being carried off to some Utopian existence, which never existed, but a normal courtship with a local boy followed by a marriage or moving in together was almost certainly the reality: having to buy a house; raising a family. Couple of kids maybe?

Then she thought of Alan, the boy — the man? — she had slept with. That was the kind of relationship she had unwittingly expected; one that ended in a more prosaic way. But now she was on a roller coaster ride for which she wasn't prepared, and she wasn't sure it was one she wanted.

Those thoughts, interspersed with moments of sleep, ran through her head until they were coming in to land at Heathrow. She had tried bravely to put them out of her mind, but with little success. Now there were other things to occupy her mind, and one of those was seeing her friend, Sue, and telling her everything.

They were standing at the luggage carousel when Simon suddenly pulled out his phone and put it to his ear. Jenny watched as his facial expression changed. He swore and cut the call, then turned to Jenny.

"That was Harry. Our father's had a heart attack." He tilted his head back. "Shit!" Then he looked at Jenny again. "He's in St. Richard's. I'll go there directly. Drop you off at yours if that's okay?"

"Oh my God, I'm so sorry, Simon. No, don't worry about me; Sue has promised to meet me. We'll get the train."

He nodded as his case came by on the carousel. He yanked it off and gave Jenny a kiss on the cheek. "I'll see you soon. 'Bye."

She watched him hurry away and wondered if this would change anything. She knew it shouldn't, but with the way she'd been thinking...

Sue was there in the arrivals lounge and squealed with delight when she saw Jenny walking through. They grabbed each other and practically danced as they cuddled and wriggled with excitement. Then Sue stood back.

"Where's Simon?"

Jenny explained. "Once he'd got his case, he wanted to be off. I'm surprised you didn't see him come through."

"Good thing I didn't," Sue said. "That would have made me wonder what he done with you."

Jenny hooked her hand around Sue's arm. "Come on," she said, "I've got loads to tell you."

***

By the time they'd reached London, Jenny had almost run out of things to say. She talked virtually non-stop, keeping Sue entertained with a blow by blow account of the last ten days where her life had taken a completely different turn, and each day just seemed to be more spectacular the previous one.

Until she began talking about the flight home.

189

They were having a coffee and toasted bun at Victoria before their train to Chichester was due to depart. Jenny's manner had changed from one of high excitement and drama to one more taciturn and measured.

"Do you really feel like that?" Sue asked. "That you want to finish with him?"

Jenny was sitting forward, resting her elbows on the table, her cup in both hands. "Oh, I don't know. When Anna came up with the idea of me going to America, I almost wet myself with excitement. I so wanted to see Simon and tell him how much I loved him — I was bursting." She laughed briefly. "But somehow, the excitement levels seemed artificial. You know, affected, put on."

"By Simon?"

"God no; he was always in control. It was me; I was like a bloody child." She put the cup down. "I didn't mind being like that, but it had to end." She laughed again. "I couldn't go on like that."

"What about Simon? Did he change?"

"No, but the strangest thing happened. When I asked him on the aeroplane what would happen to Cinderella now, he said she would go back to washing dishes."

Sue gasped in horror, her mouth wide open. "Really?"

Jenny nodded. "Yep."

"I thought Cinderella ended up marrying Prince Charming?"

Jenny grinned lopsidedly. She lowered her head and started crying softly. Sue passed her a tissue, which Jenny grabbed and wiped her face. She straightened up after a few seconds and breathed in deeply, bad moment forgotten.

"I don't think it's going to happen. In fact, one of the reasons I started feeling odd about the whole thing was that we never broached the subject of marriage."

"No proposal?"

"No."

"But the letter? His declaration of love. Can't live without you. Just bullshit?"

"I don't know, Sue. Perhaps in a week or two, we'll meet up and he'll ask me to marry him."

"But you don't want to now, do you."

Jenny sighed deeply. "Oh, I don't fucking know." She glanced at her watch. "Come on, Sue, time to go. Perhaps I'll have changed my mind when we get to Chichester."

Sue gave Jenny a peculiar look. "Perhaps I should start writing Romance instead of Children's Books. At least I would be able to start with two grown up children."

They were both laughing as they wandered away from the café in search of the platform that would take them both back to a world of reality and away from a world of fantasy.

Chapter 31

It took Jenny precisely one day at the café to find her life had returned to normal. Motty was delighted to see her and wanted to know everything of course, but she had a job to do and business was brisk, so it was towards the end of the day when she was able to sit and talk about her whirlwind days in New York. She had to give the edited version to Motty and leave the rest to his fertile imagination. But as she recalled the treasured moments, she began to feel the happiness that underpinned the time spent with Simon, and that screwed the thoughts she'd had and about which she'd spoken to Sue. She mentioned this to Motty.

"I can understand that," he said. "You've been on a fantastic high, completely different to anything you've done before. It was like drug to you my darling, and now you're coming down and suffering withdrawal symptoms. Your body has probably been living on adrenalin and now it's craving for it." He touched her on her arm. "Well, maybe not that severe, but you do need to see that. Your life will balance itself out after a couple of days."

"I haven't called Simon yet. I don't have his phone number."

"Has he called you?"

She shook her head. "No, not yet. He's probably worrying too much about his father. Maybe things have got worse."

Motty agreed. "Yes, that could be true, but I'm sure he will calls. Trust me."

She smiled. She loved Motty's optimism. "Oh, how was Anna? Was she okay?"

He put up his hand and half closed his eyes. "Oh,

absolute murder. She could wait on tables okay, but she wouldn't stop nagging me and telling where I was going wrong."

Jenny laughed. "Why didn't you fire her?"

"I couldn't my darling. I love her too much and she needs the money." He even grinned at that.

Jenny could imagine the clash of temperaments and the sibling rivalry, but she knew how close the two of them were.

"I'll have to call her; say thank you. You'll have to give me her phone number though."

He tutted and banged his eyes. Then he pulled out his phone and sent Anna's number to Jenny.

"There, my darling. I don't have Simon's though, so you'll have to ask Anna for it." He touched her again. "But I'm sure he will call." He pushed himself up from the table. "Now I must go; lots to do. See you tomorrow?"

"Of course, Motty, And thanks for the chat."

She opened her phone and put Simon's number in her contacts list. She was tempted to give him a call but thought better of it and put the phone back in her bag. Then she made her way out of the café and into the precinct. It was dark, the sun had long gone and now the temperature was dropping rapidly. She thought of New York and started walking home.

***

Simon was sitting beside his father's hospital bed at the Queen Alexandra Hospital in Portsmouth. It was known locally as the QA. Harry was with him. His father was expecting to be released that day, and the brothers were there to take him home.

"You've made up your mind then?" his father asked

193

Simon.

"Yes."

His father nodded, his head moving up and down in small, hardly noticeable movements. He looked thoughtful.

"Was it because of this?" he asked, tapping his chest.

Simon smiled. "No, you old bugger, it wasn't. My future depends on other people, other influences, not the condition of your heart."

"And young Jenny is the reason?"

It was Simon's turn to nod his head."

"Well, I hope it turns out to be the right choice. For all our sakes."

"Don't include yourself in that, Dad," Harry said to him. "You're finished with Trojan; there's no way you can go back or even contemplate going back. You know what the consultant said."

His father chuckled. "What does the bloody consultant know?"

And at that moment, a nurse came into the ward and walked over to the bedside. She was carrying a small bag which she placed on the locker top beside the bed,

"Your prescription, Mr. Daines. Instructions are in there. Now, if you get yourself dressed, I'll have a porter wheel you out."

"We can take him," Simon said.

The nurse shook her head. "Hospital policy. The Porter will be through with the wheelchair in ten minutes."

The brothers watched her walk away with amused expressions on their faces. They pulled the curtains round the bed and helped get their father dressed. Twenty minutes later they were fighting the traffic as they negotiated their way on to the A27 and home.

"You coming back with us, Simon?" Harry asked as he drove up the slip road on to the dual carriageway.

Simon shook his head. "No, drop me off at my place. I'll catch up with you and dad later."

***

Jenny hurried up the stairs into her room, shut the door behind her and dropped her coat on to the foot of the bed. Then she took her phone out of her bag and checked for any messages. There were none. That seemed to disappoint her more than anything. She tossed the phone on to the bed and slipped her shoes off. She thought about phoning for a takeaway meal but shoved that idea to the back of her mind for a while. She made a coffee for herself and opened up her laptop. Time, she thought, to consider her future. As much as she enjoyed working for Motty, she realised she needed something more. In her heart she knew what that something was, but since she heard nothing from Simon, she guessed that was now no longer an option.

She heard the sound of knocking on the front door downstairs. Her heart flipped. Then she heard voices: two people talking. Her heart stopped flipping and she went back to her laptop.

She couldn't concentrate on the screen because someone was coming up the stairs. More than two people.

She frowned as someone knocked softly on the door.

"Jenny. Do you know someone called Simon —"

"Fuck, yes!" she shouted and tossed her laptop aside as she jumped off the bed and ran to the door. She yanked it open to see Simon standing there.

"What do I have to do to see you? It's like getting into Fort Knox here." He grinned and stepped into the room and into Jenny's arms.

When they managed to unclench themselves, they flopped on to the bed.

"I thought you'd dumped me for some reason." Jenny told him.

He propped himself up on his elbow. "No way. I'm sorry I neglected you, Jenny, but it was touch and go with my dad. I spent most of my time up at the QA."

"Oh, my God. Is he okay?"

"Yes. We brought him home this afternoon. He's fine." He shifted a little, bringing himself round so he was leaning over Jenny. "Will you marry me?"

Jenny's mouth fell open. She couldn't speak for a few seconds. Then she pulled him towards her. "Yes, yes. Fuck, yes!"

She started crying as she tried to kiss him. She could feel his tears on her face as they embraced.

"Oh, Simon," she murmured as they pulled themselves apart.

He sat up. "I was going to propose to you when we got back from New York. I had it all planned in my head. A romantic dinner at a quiet place. Nice and intimate. But then my father buggered all that up."

He sat up and got off the bed and on to his knees. "I know I've asked and you've said yes, but I forgot to show you this." He brought a small box from his pocket and flipped it open.

Jenny stared at the diamond ring, looked at Simon and then she couldn't see anything because her eyes were filled with tears.

He slipped the ring on her finger. "Jenny, my darling, I love you. Will you marry me?"

"Oh you are a silly sod, Simon, but I love you for it."

She splayed her fingers out and admired the ring. "Wait till I tell Sue; she'll be over the moon for me."

"KJ?"

She took her eyes off the ring and glanced at him. "Probably, but not over the moon enough to take me back."

"Is that what you want?"

She shrugged and looked back at the ring. "I did make up my mind that I needed to think about, well, more than working at the café, as much as I like the job." She forced herself to drop her hand and look at Simon.

"And what about you? Back to Trojan's?"

He shook his head. "No; I've decided my life needs to change direction too. I spoke to Guy Ford. Told him of my decision."

Jenny's face fell. "But Simon, you loved that job."

"Yes, but as a single man it was a very fulfilling job. But then I realised that to be married to you, live with you, grow old with you, was all I wanted."

"But will you be happy? You'll still have your big house —"

He stopped her by putting the tips of his fingers on her lips. "Not anymore; I've given it to Harry and Anna." He could see the surprised look on her face. "As a wedding present."

"Oh my goodness. Are they getting married?"

"It wouldn't be a wedding present if they weren't," he said.

"Oh, funny man. When did this happen?"

"While you and I were in New York. Harry proposed to her on New Year's Eve."

"So here will you live?"

"With you."

"Here? In this dump?"

He took her hands in his. "I have a flat in Chichester. I want you to come and live with me there."

Jenny's heart was beginning to beat a little quicker. "Simon, this is all too much. It's, I don't know, all this wonderful news at once."

He was still on his knees. He straightened, reached up to her and cupped his hands around her face.

"Do you love me?"

"Yes."

"Will you come and live with me?"

"Yes."

"How long will it take you to pack?"

"Ten minutes."

He stood up. "Make it twenty; there's something I want to do."

She looked shocked. "Here?"

He pushed her gently. "At this moment I can't think of a better time and a better place."

She managed to reach the bedside light switch and plunged the room into darkness. Today was definitely the start of the best days in her life.

Epilogue

No, Simon didn't change his mind and go back to Trojan after all, despite Jenny trying to persuade him; he bought the gym instead. The owner, Benson, agreed to run the place while Simon studied at the local college to become a personal trainer.

Jenny moved into his flat and started changing it from an austere, bog standard bachelor pad to one that bit by bit improved with some nice, feminine touches. He didn't object; he became quite fascinated with the way Jenny was slowly changing him in a way only a woman could.

Jenny didn't leave Motty's employment. She found she was so content with life now that she knew she had found her Shangri la. Simon was so pleased for her. So was Motty.

Anna and Harry got married. The announcement surprised a lot of people. Simon was best man, while Jenny and Sue were asked to be bridesmaids. It was a plush do, lots of important people from the motor racing world were there. The three women had a wonderful time touring round the specialist wedding shops.

Motty was asked to give Anna away. He was beside himself with the sheer joy of being able to parade himself in front of all those people. The suit he wore was the latest thing from a top designer in London.

KJ was there too. She had been asked about linking up with Trojan again, but turned them down: once bitten, twice shy as she told Simon.

Motty and Julian decided to launch out and bought the lease on a building next to the café. The plan was to extend the café and turn it into more of a restaurant serving meals well into the late evening. Motty wanted it to become one of the finest places in town and asked Jenny if she would oversee the entire project. He promoted her to his so-called 'Chief of staff' and pitched in with a pay rise. She still waited on tables but was now in charge of three waiters and a kitchen hand.

And life rolled on, sometimes frantically, sometimes peacefully and sometimes popping up with little surprises—

Like the day Jenny announced she was pregnant.

The End

Author note

Emma Carney is the pen name of multi-genre author, Michael Parker. You can learn more about Michael and his books by visiting www.michaelparkerbooks.com.

If you enjoyed this story, please leave a review, or simply tell your reader friends about it. Reviews and word of mouth can be so helpful to a writer.

Thank you.

Michael Parker

Printed in Great Britain
by Amazon

18472237R00119